Walking up a Slide

Copyright © 2014 by Daley James Fra

www.DaleyJFrancis.com

Cover Design © 2014 Peter O'Connor

www.BespokeBookCovers.com

All rights reserved. This book or any portion thereof may not be reproduced or used in any manner whatsoever without the express written permission of the author except for the use of brief quotations in a book review.

The right of Daley James Francis to be identified as the author of this work has been asserted in accordance with the Copyright, Designs & Patents Act 1988.

All characters in this novel are fictitious. Any resemblance to actual events, locales or persons, living or dead, is entirely coincidental.

ISBN-13: 978-1500878375

Contents

1. What is Love? — 3
2. Home is Where Your Friends Are — 21
3. The One That Got Away — 35
4. The Invite — 48
5. Pictures of Lila — 66
6. The Voices of Reason — 86
7. Drink To Forget — 105
8. The Breakfast Club — 122
9. From Despair to Where? — 138
10. Plus One, Twice, Three Times a Lady — 156
11. Emotional Maturity — 174
12. Squeaky Bum Time — 190
13. Nice Day for a Shite Wedding — 206
14. The Reunion — 224
15. Coming to Terms — 236
16. One Door Closes… — 248
    Acknowledgements — 266

1. What is Love?

Love.

For some people, it's hell. For others, it simply never comes. And for people like me, it's a Coldplay song playing over the scene in the movie where the romantic lead skips off into the night knowing that everything is going to be OK.

My name is Jason Chapman, and I will be your hero, baby.

I grew up watching a ridiculous amount of movies, and I clung desperately to the notion that when you got the girl and the credits started to roll, everything was going to be hunky dory. When you think like this, you're opening yourself up to a world of hurt.

My home town is the perfect place for a kid to develop unrealistic ideals for what love is. It is the kind of place David Lynch would have used as an inspiration for *Blue Velvet*: White picket fences and freshly mown lawns on the surface, before you got to the dark underbelly where Dennis Hopper was lurking with a gas mask and a pair of scissors.

Maybe that's being a little over-dramatic.

Dennis Hopper has never visited my home town.

I spent most of my childhood with my head in the clouds. I watched a ridiculous amount of films and read every book I could get my hands on. Dad had no idea – or didn't care – about film classification or censorship, so the first films I watched growing up were the likes of *The Terminator* and *The Fly,* much to the horror of my mum, who took care of the Disney side of things for damage control purposes. If I go through life without murdering anyone, mum will have succeeded. Although she did let me watch *Watership Down,* which probably ruined me more than Arnie punching through a thug's stomach. Thanks, Mum.

I like to think that I'm a good looking guy. At school, I looked like a shorter, slightly rounder version of a *Parklife*-era Alex James, on account of the curtains. By the time I went to college, I was madly in man-love with James Dean Bradfield, and copied everything from his hairstyle, dress sense and even the way he played guitar. OK, so it was air guitar, but don't judge me. I'm good at it.

These days, I look like James Dean Bradfield if he gave up being the coolest man in the history of music, started working in a hotel and lived on takeaways, beer, cheap coffee and processed shite. Once my metabolism catches up with me, I'm going to be in big trouble. But for now, I'll continue to ride my luck in style.

The brown hair-blue eyes combo served me well at school, college and continues to do so to this day, even if it is with my mums friends rather than ladies my own age. But that's OK, as I prefer the mature lady.

My GCSE results read like a song sheet: a scattering of C's, D's, E's and F's, and a G in there to give it some added flavour. My friends and I discussed the next step as we left the school. The plans comprised of: blag our way into college, do Leisure and Tourism because it'd be easy, and then go and live in Ibiza for ten years and earn our stripes.

I'd never blagged my way into anything my entire life. However, when it came time to enrol at college, the tutor seemed to take a shine to me. I told her what I'd like to do, and that my GCSE's were an accurate portrayal of my laziness, but not my intelligence. I just needed to feel something in my gut in order to fully apply myself. Before I left the building, I was on the course.

College was amazing. I didn't have a clue as to what I wanted to do with my life, but at least I'd have my best friends around for another two years at least, and there was a good chance that I'd meet a girl and we'd live happily ever after.

You know that episode of *Red Dwarf* where Lister meets his younger self and wants to give him a good hard slap? I'd love that opportunity. You see, by the time I turned 18, my idealistic view of love and relationships was torn to shreds. I realised that, when you let someone into your heart, jealousy, distrust and confusion come to the party, and they're the kind of guests who get drunk and inappropriately touch people before vomiting on the sofa and passing out in a flower-bed.

I graduated with a 'Pass' in my GNVQ (Generally Not Very Qualified) in Leisure and Tourism, but the next phase of my life didn't plan out quite as I'd imagined it would. I was single, university wasn't an option and getting a job didn't seem as sexy as travelling or becoming a holiday rep in Ibiza, which was the reason I'd signed up to Leisure and Tourism in the first place. As a naïve 16 year old about to reach new depths of mediocrity in his GCSE's, I came across *Ibiza Uncovered* – a show where a bunch of excitable but unspectacular Brits go over to the island of partying and get paid to get pissed, dance to awful music and pull girls. It seemed like a great career opportunity. My careers advisor had told me to work in a supermarket. No offence to Rita on the checkout, but getting girls into nightclubs seemed like a better proposition.

The problem with teenage dreams is that they are based on TV shows that soon become terrible. The people in *Ibiza Uncovered* had become dull and pathetic to me. They were repeating the same tricks, only the alcohol had made them bloated and spotty, which wasn't a great selling point to a teenager. The problem with this realisation was that it was made one year into my course. At least I was with my friends, I thought.

Twelve months later, they were gone too. They all went to university, although one of them dropped out when his girlfriend got pregnant. Sounds like the opening of a Bryan Adams song, but it's the truth. The ignorance of youth is a beautiful thing, but dangerous. I pinned my hopes on us being inseparable and going on an adventure together. By the end of my teens, these hopes were buried under a mountain of parental questions like "What are you going to do next?"

"Fuck knows," was the answer to that.

The day I finished college was worse than picking up those disastrous GCSE results. When you're 16, you don't care about the future, you're just happy to be alive and be with your mates, who are as ridiculous as you are. But when you finish college at 18, the weight or expectation bears down on you, but hopefully you've become a little wiser in the ways of love and friendship, usually as a result of having your heart pulled out of your arse.

The next step was to find something called a 'career'. Whatever that means.

I moved to Leicester in the summer of 2000, and got a job at the Hunters Hotel on a Hospitality Management trainee scheme that involved working in every department of the hotel for two months at a time, before settling down as Duty Manager.

The Duty Manager was a dogsbody in all but name, but it was good fun, and by the end of the scheme, I had seen every shade of weird. Some people enter a hotel and it's a gateway to another world, where you're allowed to behave like a rock star who's recovering from crack addiction.

My first shift as a Duty Manager saw me have to wake up a local rugby team so they could meet a bus at 7am. Bearing in mind my shift *started* at 7am and most of these rugby lads had only been back from a night on the lash for a couple of hours, it wasn't surprising that this was what I found in each of the seven rooms I visited on my wakeup call:

Room 1 – Two grown men in bed together, covered in each other's vomit

Room 2 – Empty

Room 3 – One drunk, naked man crying on his bed, twisting his wedding ring on his finger as he rocked back and forth

Room 4 – A still-drunk 6 foot 8 man-mountain who told me to fuck off before throwing a boot at my head

Room 5 – One man, two prostitutes

Room 6 – A snoring mammoth who had to be woken up with a glass of water over the face (administered by a helpful Housekeeper so that I wouldn't get beaten to death)

Room 7 – A polite young man who was fully dressed and thanked me for coming to see him.

It was a baptism of fire, but for five years, that was my working life. Swanning around a hotel in a nice suit, holding a walkie-talkie, helping each department out and smiling as I went. I worked 60-70 hours a week for shit pay and even less thanks, but it was a good enough craic.

Weddings were the best. One day somebody will make a fly-on-the-wall documentary about what *really* happens at a wedding. There's nothing quite like it. Pure chaos. Everyone is angry, bitter, jealous, bored or harbouring a secret that comes out after four pints of Guinness and two whisky's, threatening to destroy both sides of the family before the evening ends.

The beauty of it was that I had front row seats and didn't have to pay for a ticket. If you were a screenwriter and wrote down half the scenes I'd witnessed at weddings, Hollywood would turn you away for being OTT.

The first wedding I ever supervised was an Indian wedding, where there were no drinks and everything was expected to be smoother than a baby's backside. But naturally, being my first one in charge, it was an unprecedented disaster…

After the nuptials, we noticed the two families were sat on opposite sides of the room and were just staring at each other, like the two gangs from *West Side Story*. We were waiting for everybody to break into dance, when we found out that five minutes previously, the Best Man had kindly informed the groom that not only was he in love with the bride, but he had shagged her last night.

In the wedding suite.

In his bed.

Suffice to say, the atmosphere was tense. The cliché of "cutting the atmosphere with a knife" didn't apply here. You would have needed a fucking machete.

The poor groom was discouraged from doing anything silly by his doting parents and the evening went by without any deaths, but it was easily the tensest evening I've ever witnessed, like watching the "Funny how?" scene from *Goodfellas* but drawn out to over six hours instead of thirty seconds. Excruciating. All I kept thinking was, 'How is the bride just sitting there with a smile on her face?' It must have sapped her of every ounce of energy not to burst into tears or go running to the safety of her wedding bed. If I ever wanted to try and pinpoint the exact moment I became cynical about the notion of marriage, that was it.

Five years of working at the hotel had slowly chipped away at the naïve boy who believed in love and romance, with my view edging more towards the ending of *The Graduate,* rather than every Jennifer Aniston movie ever made.

On the plus side of things, at least my career was working out. Craig, a handsome thirty-eight-year-old Edinburgh native who moved to Leicester because there were too many English people in Scotland, was my superior. A brute force of tough love and C-bombs, Craig was exactly the kind of mentor I needed to stop myself from turning to the dark side. He kept me focussed, energised and – a lot of the time – drunk. As the Food and Beverage Manager, Craig had devised a number of ways to keep his staff onside and the Manager's happy. In short, he screwed people over to ensure the stocktakes were great, and made sure the stock-takers never left empty handed when they came to do their thing.

From a staff point of view, when a busy shift ended and everybody had worked hard, you could place your bets that Craig would make you feel appreciated.

He first showed this side to me after a particularly tough DM shift. The reception team had managed to fuck up their own rota and not have enough staff on, which meant yours truly was getting radio calls every two seconds for menial tasks like taking soap and extra towels to bedrooms. Craig watched me do it, then sat me down and fed me some of his wisdom, washed down with a cold pint of Grolsch.

"It's been a long night," he said. "But it'd be a lot shorter if you learnt how to deal with those reception girls."

"How do you mean?" I asked.

"As soon as you hear the words 'Hello Jason' over that radio, you're on your way. You've got to make them understand that unless they *really* need you, they can get fucked."

"I'm not that bad, am I?"

"Not yet, but they see you as a soft touch right now. They blamed the rota for the fact that they used you to do these tasks, but if the bar or the restaurant was busy, do would they call you? Nah, they graft it out. Those lazy fuckers need to do the same thing and stop taking the easy route."

"How did you stop them doing it?"

"On my first day, I switched the radio off and crept around the back office. They were sitting around texting their mates and scratching their backsides, and I appeared out of nowhere and said, 'You call me again for anything that isn't an evacuation of the entire hotel and I will skull-fuck the lot of you'. Now they don't do it. Or look at me. Perfect."

As terrifying and brutal as that sounded, the guy had a point, and that's why the top managers never read Craig the riot act if anyone started crying as a result of his often-cruel tirades. He got results, and he achieved them by working his arse off and ensuring everyone else did the same. You couldn't really argue with that.

"Take Mike, for example,"

Craig *loved* Mike, another DM who was similar to a puppy; excitable and eager to please, to the point of desperation.

"He's so nice and obedient and pathetic that he's got the mobile numbers of almost everyone in the hotel. That makes it personal. Now he gets called to take ironing boards up to rooms when the hotel isn't even busy…"

"I don't do that!"

"I know. But it's a slippery slope. Give them a mile and they'll take a marathon. There has to be a moment when you say, 'Right, that's it' and give it to them with both barrels. But you reward the guys that work hard and don't take the piss."

"With Grolsch?"

"With Grolsch."

I tapped Craig's glass with mine, and watched as Johnny, the night porter, came by to fix some drinks for some late arrivals. Craig turned around and raised his glass to the old codger.

"Get yourself a Grolsch, Johnny," Craig said.

"Thanks, Craig."

Johnny approached the bar with an added spring in his step and started making the drinks. Craig looked at me, knowing that he'd made his point well.

"Any man who has to endure this place five nights a week when he's in his sixties deserves a beer."

"Reward?"

"Exactly."

"There's hope for your soul yet, Craig."

"It's just a shame that it's soaked in gin."

Craig's other claim to fame was that he had slept with someone in four out of the five conference rooms at the hotel. I suggested that he might as well take his girlfriend there to complete the set, but he said that was too easy, and with the teacher's conference coming up, the time of his greatest achievement was at hand. Most people would be disgusted at such a sexist conquest – which meant cheating on his long-term girlfriend – but like Tyler Durden, Craig made being a bastard acceptable somehow. If I had tried to do something like that, I'd be hung drawn and quartered for it. Everybody knew Craig was a shitbag. It was expected of him.

When Craig wasn't working, I spent most of my shifts avoiding work for as long as possible. If I hadn't been twenty-three years old, with the face of a fourteen-year-old boy band member, I would've been found out a long time ago. The Management liked me because I looked good in a suit and people in general liked me, which meant that angry, drunk or complaining guests were disarmed with relative ease. If Craig had a drunk customer in his face, they would be psychologically maimed to within an inch of their lives before being thrown out by Ben the Bouncer, a fat guy with a David Brent goatee, who would often sit at the end of the bar and drink 40 pints of Diet Coke in three hours until he resembled a bloated, pregnant seal.

My main hangout was the coffee machine at the bar. It had a blind spot from the security cameras, and it came with the added bonus of being Jane's humble abode. Jane was a sweet, cuddly ball of maternal love who would ply me with espressos until my eyes popped out of my head. At the start of every early shift, I would shoot the breeze with Jane before checking each floor of the hotel for room service trays, vomit and dead bodies.

"One espresso for sir," Jane would say as she dropped a tiny cup filled with brown heaven on the work surface.

"You're a legend, Jane. I suppose I should keep walking?"

"Unless you *want* to do some work?"

"That would render you jobless. I would never forgive myself."

I dropped the espresso down the hatch and left the comfort zone of the coffee machine, feeling the slight sting of a bar towel as it whipped my backside, courtesy of Jane. A job like this only keeps its appeal if the staff are characters, and there were plenty of those scattered around the hotel. They were the reason I came in at all. I saw the potential in them, and they saw my backside at the Christmas party. Fair trade.

The next check-in was the kitchen. Sai, a chunky Indian chef in his late forties with a Freddie Mercury moustache, had the only computer outside of the back office. The others were occupied by the sales and reservations girls, which meant Sai's computer was the Holy Grail, and if you scanned the internet history, the pit of hell.

I visited Sai's office every morning to get the daily report, as the DM couldn't attend the early management meetings in case an emergency occurred, such as somebody setting off the fire alarm or calling in a bomb threat. The second one actually happened once, but it was just a disgruntled ex-employee who had taken acid and decided to prank call every number on his phone pretending to be a terrorist. Proof that drugs are only harmful when used by idiots, he's now serving a three year prison sentence. What a bellend.

The daily report included any VIP guests who were staying at the hotel, and the biggest pain was Mr Loury, a businessman originally from Pakistan who spent far too much time in the East Midlands.

This guy was a mystery to me. He would complain about *everything* and still tip through the roof. He once spent 20 minutes complaining to me about his bedside lamp not working, which I could have gone up and fixed in a quarter of that time, before handing me £20 for assuring him that it would be fixed by the time he came back from work.

Craig despised Loury, and made it his mission to piss him off whenever the opportunity arose. Despite this, Loury was the main reason that the majority of the F&B staff would kill for Craig, as Loury had inadvertently paid for the unofficial staff party. When Loury's son got married at the hotel, Craig was trusted with Loury's credit card, and told to "Cut it off when it hit £3,000." The tab for Loury's guests came to about £1,000 worth of drinks. The rest of the budget went on wine, spirits and copious amounts of Grolsch for all of us. To this day, Loury knows nothing about the debauchery that he funded, but we thank him for it in our prayers every night.

When Craig read the daily report and saw the word 'Loury', a sinister smile appeared on his face.

"What are you smiling at?" I asked.

"I drank two bottles of red wine with my curry last night. When Loury goes to work, I'm going to take the nastiest shit in his toilet. Might accidentally remove the air freshener as well. You enjoy your day."

Once I had read the daily report, the next step was to head to the back office and speak to George Walters, the General Manager. The GM was OK, but like all top managers, they could save a baby from a burning building and all the guys on £6 an hour would still think they're a cunt.

He didn't help the situation. He would walk up to the bar while it was packed with customers and the staff were sweating blood, and ask them to make sure the ashtrays were emptied. There was nothing more patronising – not to mention demeaning – than an idiot with a suit and a degree but no grafting experience completely missing the point of how their business actually ran.

The GM and I would take a walk through the hotel lobby, talking about the events of the day and making sure that each department was prepared. Although he was a 9-5 suit working in a hotel environment, the GM had a pretty good eye for detail. He could walk through the lobby and spot something that nobody else had noticed, like a light bulb that had gone out or a mark on the wall. He knew his hotel well, but not the people working in it. That's the price of being the guy at the top, I guess. But he liked me and wanted to see me progress.

In truth though, the job was getting stale. I loved the people, and Craig kept me on my toes, but something needed to change. In the hotel industry, you only get promoted when someone dies or moves on. But it wasn't the place that was the problem for me; it *was* me. I had no long-term plan. It was like GCSE results day all over again, but it's not as sexy to be a directionless fool when you're twenty-three.

The main issue was that my job had become my social life, something Craig had warned me about but I hadn't heeded his warning. I had killed any realistic chance of getting a girlfriend unless I worked with her, which was an unofficial rule of mine: don't have a fling or get into a relationship with a colleague. It would be doomed to fail from the start. It was bad enough working stupid hours in the place already, but living out our private lives at the same time? Nah.

It was time to branch out from the confines of my job and start dating again, but I had no idea how to do that. I'd been out of the game for a long time, and had only been on two dates in the last year.

The first one was when I went to the pub with a friend and started chatting to an Australian girl behind the bar. We went out for something to eat after her shift ended and we had a bit of a fumble, and that was the end of that. Working shifts guaranteed that our diaries never synchronised, which meant any hope of a relationship fizzled out quickly. People tend to stop asking you out after you've turned them down a dozen times.

The second date was set up by Mum, which was a little embarrassing, but nowhere near as bad as the date itself. Emma was new to Leicester, and she had worked for mum for a bit. Mum tried to do a nice thing and set us up, but it didn't go well.

Imagine pulling all of your teeth out, then replacing them with salt crystals. It was that painful. I kept trying to force the conversation, but all I got was one word answers. Not only was Emma mute, but she chain-smoked too. Of all my bugbears, smoking is the worst. You might as well let an animal nest in your mouth. It would have the same effect on me: Instant loss of interest.

Two weeks after the date, mum told me that Emma was gutted I didn't call her again. I will never understand the opposite sex.

2. Home is Where Your Friends Are

Jim and Sean were my two best friends, and they were the two most different people you could ever meet. Jim and I went to secondary school together, and all he had ever wanted to do was join the army. He watched war films, read books and magazines filled with tanks, war stories and god knows what else, and was hell-bent on joining at 16. There was no Plan B.

Sometimes I imagine what he would have done if he'd been turned away. I think he would have become Mike from *Spaced,* only thinner and more homicidal. Saying that, I remember catching him crying at *Ghost,* so maybe I'm being too quick to judge.

I admired Jim for being so focused and bloody-minded in his career. I had drifted all over the place and had no idea where I'd be in five years. Jim knew exactly where he'd be: shooting people and disabling bombs in a faraway land, or playing Xbox in my living room. Either way, the British Army would be paying him a salary. That was pretty cool.

At school, Jim terrified most people. The product of a broken family who had little money, Jim was the happiest kid I knew. There were kids with perfect families who moped around and whinged about how unfair life was, but Jim would smile through a funeral. I think it made a lot of people uncomfortable, but it was what first drew me towards him. I like people who weren't just what they appear to be on the surface, and on Jim's surface, he was the stereotypical squaddie: brash, cocky and more than a little sexist. But for a guy with such a rampant libido and an apparent lack of respect for women and other people's relationships, I had never seen someone pour so much love and attention on a sibling. Jim's little sister Faye was his pride and joy. He was a beautiful mass of contradictions.

Jim had lived with me for 18 months, ever since he had seized the opportunity to work at the army recruitment centre in Leicester. He saw this as an opportunity to indulge in the uni lifestyle he'd missed out on. One day, he turned up at my door and announced that he was moving in. It was like the opening scene of a sitcom, only the laughing track was just my own nervous laughter, and I figured that he had done a Van Damme and gone AWOL for some reason. I thought it better not to ask about it.

Jim's only belongings were a sports bag filled with clothes, his army uniform and a framed picture of his regiment from the day they had met the Queen Mother. It soon transpired that the army had actually offered him accommodation, but he turned it down so he could live with me, his best friend.

Since living with me, Jim had put a few pounds on around the waistline. Nothing to us civilians, but to Jim, it was torture. He'd say that we were making him soft, but before long, we'd be sharing pizza and beers. I was delighted to be contributing something to the British Army, even if was an out-of-shape squaddie with a drinking problem.

Jim and I first bonded over our love of films, and the fact that I was the only kid at school who wasn't terrified or weirded out by him. We would re-enact scenes from *Full Metal Jacket*, taking it in turns to be Gunnery Sergeant Hartman and the recruits. It was a lot of fun, if you were a geek like us. If you weren't, it looked like *One Flew Over the Cuckoo's Nest: The School Years*.

If you were writing a remake of *The Odd Couple* and wanted the absolute polar opposite of Jim, you would come up with Sean, my other housemate. Apart from the alcohol intake, Sean had nothing at all in common with Jim, but found him funny and interesting in a documentary-on-serial-killers kind of way. I think Sean was waiting for the day that Jim finally broke and became a Chuck Norris character, but sadly it never happened.

Sean worked in holiday sales full-time, but his dream job was to manage a football team. He was working his way towards it, taking FA courses and leading a local under-14s team to glory in the league and cup for the last two years straight. Jim and I would often go to watch the kids train on a Thursday, and listen to them bantering away with each other as Sean put them through their paces.

Sean was the ultimate beer monster. He worked hard, but as soon as it came time to cut loose, he did so with aplomb. If you tried to keep up with him, you'd wake up the next morning filled with pain and regret, with the emotional and physical scars to show for it. I once walked into the bathroom to find Jim fully-uniformed in the shower, covered in vomit. He had no idea how he got there or why he was doing it, but the last thing he remembered was Sean suggesting they "have a few beers".

Sean and I met on the last day of secondary school. I was picking up my GCSE results, and Sean had just moved to the area. His parents introduced him to my friend Will, who lived on the same street. Will knew that I would be a good fit for Sean, and he was right. We clicked right away.

On the same day, Jim broke into the leisure centre and stole two boxes of Mars ice creams, and spent the last hour of school giving 144 Mars bars out to people, like a young Willy Wonka. Sean thought this was hilarious, and a bond was formed.

That night, we sat on top of the hill in the big park and drank several warm cans of Fosters. It tasted like piss, but we didn't care. The world was our oyster.

Cut to five years later, and Sean had been living with me and Jim for the past six months, after his relationship with Georgie broke down. Sean was amazing at his sales job, and had bought a house at 18 years of age, which to me was insane, but when he sold the house and made £40,000 profit just before moving in with us, I changed my opinion. The problem for Sean was that he had traded in his house and relationship for a fat cheque and sharing a home with two idiots.

Sean had prepared himself for the beer-monster life, but then he met Georgie, and fell in love with her instantly. She domesticated him right away, without him even realising it, and from the ages of 17-22, Sean was a hard-working guy with a house, girlfriend and a dog. Then one day, Georgie came home from work and used the words "marriage" and "children" in the same sentence, and suddenly the house was on the market and my rent was one-third cheaper. When I asked why he gave up on Georgie, he simply said: "You either meet someone at the right time or the wrong time, and it was ten years early for me."

I knew where he was coming from, but it didn't stop me thinking that he'd made a huge mistake. But out of love for my friend, I took Sean to Benidorm for a week after Georgie left. I like to think that it was fun for him, even if he did spend seven days on a conveyor belt of lap dances, Tequila, and crying into his t-shirt sleeves. I indulged myself with several bouts of karaoke, but I turned my nose up at the opportunity of putting notches on the bedpost with fun-loving-yet-easy girls who wanted to use and abuse a soft-skinned fool like me. I used the excuse that I was there for my mate, but the truth was that I was fucking terrified, and haunted by a dream I had where I was raped by a hen party, and woke up with a bottle of Lambrini hanging out my arse.

Jim tried to do his bit to help Sean get over his heartbreak too. He came home from being stationed in Germany with a brand new car, and offered to take Sean and me to the Peak District to celebrate Sean's new-found independence. Unfortunately, he'd gotten used to driving on the right side of the road, and following five near misses, three bouts of road rage and two visits to a ditch, we decided to abort the trip. Instead of long walks and fresh air, we opted for no exercise and air that smelt like dead animals, by allowing Sean to drink himself into oblivion at home. We ended the night by taking Sean to a strip club, and spent all of our money keeping Sean in dances, until he was kicked out for vomiting into a girls ass crack as she performed a handstand in front of him. We had to pay another £100 for the trouble, and we didn't even get to keep the footage.

Knowing where Sean is now – both as a person and professionally – it did come too fast for him. I was the opposite: finding somebody at seventeen might have given me the focus and the drive to get my house in order, instead of fumbling my way through this half-arsed career that had prevented me from forming any kind of relationship, let alone a doomed one.

Thoughts of getting back out there filled my brain as I entered our terraced house, which smelt like stale beer, unwashed plates and farts for six days a week, before we would all get down on ourselves and have a cleaning day. We all secretly enjoyed those days though. Scrubbing can be quite therapeutic.

"Hey buddy, you look like terrible," said Jim, his back to me as he played video games on the sofa that was parked next to the front door.

"You haven't even seen me," I replied.

"The way you open the door tells me everything I need to know."

"They teach you that in the army?"

"It's a natural quirk. Slow turn of the key and quiet opening of the door means "I've had a bad day". The more noise you make generally dictates how energised and happy you are. If you burst through the door and slammed it behind you, I would assume that you'd just got laid."

"Thanks for the social study."

"You're welcome."

"Where's Sean?"

"Hiding his paedophilic tendencies behind the façade of a football coach. He's due back soon though."

It was this kind of horrific humour that made me want to introduce Jim to Craig at work, but it would probably be like crossing the streams in *Ghostbusters*. Better to keep them separated.

The second I entered my house, it was like all of my work clothes were on fire. I had to peel them off and get into joggers and a T-shirt as soon as possible. Jim likened it to the transformation scene in *An American Werewolf in London,* which was a pretty accurate and cool comparison, only I never got to shag Jenny Agutter after I'd finished eating people.

Jim threw down the Xbox control pad and turned round before I could shed my work skin. Whenever this happened, I had to be prepared for a grilling.

"What's the matter with you, buddy?" Jim asked.

"Eh?" I replied.

"You haven't seemed like yourself in a while. What's bothering you?"

This was my opportunity to open up and ask for help in finding out how to get myself back on the market, but then I decided that I might come across like Mike in *Swingers* and either a) Be ridiculed or b) Actually have to follow through with what was suggested. I chose to focus on the paused video game on the screen.

"Looks like Holyfield's got you there, big guy," I said, nodding to the screen, where Jim's *Fight Night* character was getting pummelled by Evander Holyfield.

"What? Oh, right… Yeah. I can never beat that fucker. You can't bite ears on this game."

"Every fighter I make on this game destroys Holyfield."

"I like knockouts, Larry Merchant."

"I like to keep the zero, Mr 22-5-1."

"Being undefeated is for pussies. It's the guys who come back who get my vote."

"Which Stallone film was that from?"

Jim laughed. I was safe. But then…

"How did the date go with Steph?"

Ah, Steph. The last girl I had gone on a "date" with outside of the Aussie and mum's disastrous hook-up attempt. I'd forgotten about it until Jim brought it up, like a childhood trauma. It wasn't quite as bad as that, but only because I have no idea how it ended. Let me explain…

Steph and I met when she and her mum were staying at the hotel I worked in. It was De Montfort University's graduation day, and I was chatting to them when Steph's mum suggested that I take her daughter out on her last night in Leicester. I obliged, and we headed to the city centre.

It was all going so well, but when I get nervous, I drink fast. My nerves were making me appear charming and sweet to Steph, but they were also making me skull Jack Daniels and Cokes like George Best at Happy Hour. We stepped out into the cold air and the next thing I knew, it was the next day and I was left piecing the night together like a drunk Leonard Shelby. When I woke up the next day, I was sitting upright on her sofa with my entire bottom half covered in rice.

I crept out the house and never saw her again.

Jim thought this was hilarious.

"Thanks for your support," I said.

"C'mon man, you've got to admit that's funny. Did you not get her number or anything?"

"Nope. All I can remember is her walking ahead of me as I stumbled along the road. Everything else is a mystery."

"That's amazing. It's much better to imagine the carnage. Well, not for you, obviously."

"Yeah, thanks for that."

Jim burst out laughing again, before climbing off the sofa and stretching out.

"I'm going to make you one of my boom-boom black coffees. That'll make you feel better."

"What does coffee have in common with Eric Clapton?"

The anticipation built for the punchline.

"They both suck without Cream."

Jim smirked at my joke, but at least he'd stopped laughing at me. Instead, he pointed at the Xbox controller.

"Beat Holyfield. You'll feel better."

Jim wandered off to make coffee, I thought about my unsuccessful date with Steph and considered what I could learn from it, if and when I take some poor girl out again:

Rule #1 – No drinking

Rule #2 – No involvement from mine or anyone else's mother

Rule #3 – Keep it simple.

Rule #3 was all about doing something where the stakes weren't high; cinema, bowling – something harmless and fun where I could ease myself back into being in female company outside of work, or places where booze flows.

Before I could concentrate too much on real life, I had a computerised version of four-time heavyweight champion Evander Holyfield to beat, and he was kicking my arse.

I'd managed to successfully divert Jim's attention away from my love-life and towards playing *Fight Night* for the remainder of the evening, and I crept upstairs to check my emails before bed. Before long, there was a knock on the door.

"Come in," I said.

"Is your winky away?" Sean replied.

"Yeah, you're safe."

Sean popped his head around the door before entering.

"I downloaded the entire Best Picture category at work today. Their internet connection is the tits," he said.

"I'm glad that you're doing your bit to destroy the film industry."

"Don't try and come across all Jesus to me. You'll watch the fuckers. I might never have to buy a DVD again."

"Or the FBI will track you down and you'll be sharing a cell with a 350lbs rapist called Charles for the next ten years."

"True… What are you up to? Watching porn?"

"No. Checking my emails."

"Fuck off. Just be honest. Porn is fine. I found a video the other day that had been viewed 11 million times. That's nothing to be ashamed of."

"It is when you were 10 million of those views."

"Ha-Ha. Touché. This came for you, by the way. Looks official, not like a bill."

"Cheers. Throw it on the bed."

Sean threw the envelope on the bed. Whatever it was, the only thing I had on my mind was sleep and the beginning of my quest to find a girl who wasn't mute and could keep up with my drunken rice-spilling.

I pulled myself out of my computer chair to use the toilet before bed, only to be stopped by Sean, who was shaking his head and looking serious.

"I wouldn't go out there, buddy," he said. "Jim's entertaining."

Jim *entertaining* could only ever mean absolute debauchery.

"What's he doing?" I asked, reluctantly.

"He's got some weird Goth girl round, and they're watching *Cats and Dogs.* It makes them think he's a nice guy, but then it's like Cronenberg's *Crash* in there."

"Nice."

"I'm going to bed before the film finishes and he gets his gimp mask on. Last time he had a girl round, I crossed him on the stairs and he was wearing a Spider-Man outfit with the arse cut out. Goodnight."

"Goodnight, man."

Sean slowly and quietly disappeared into the dark of the landing, tiptoeing back to his room. Sean and I often joked that Jim's bedroom was like the attic from *Hellraiser,* and we tried to preserve any sense of humanity by staying the fuck away from the place.

As the computer shut down, the room faded into darkness, and as the final glimmer of blue light faded from the screen, I glanced over to my bed, where the big shiny envelope was calling out to me.

'What the fuck is that?' I thought, like an old man who hears the phone ringing and wastes five rings wondering who it is instead of just finding out.

I picked up the envelope. The typography was stunning, like it was written with feather and ink 200 years ago. It seemed a tragic waste to tear it open and chuck it away, but I switched my bedside lamp on and tore into it anyway.

I wish I hadn't.

3. The One That Got Away

The worst part about having a terrible night's sleep is clock watching. Time seems to stand still, and your clock ticks in a mocking tone. It takes all of your energy not to smash the thing into pieces.

The source of my lack of sleep was the beautifully written and constructed envelope, and the contents thereof. I knew that it could only ever have been one of two things: a wedding invite, or the news that a rich relative I'd never met had croaked and left me millions.

As the latter was about as likely as Gary Glitter selling out Knebworth, it had to be a wedding invite.

"Dear Jason Chapman, the parents of Lila Holmes and Mark Shattersby invite you to their wedding reception on Friday 23rd June 2006 at the Hunters Hotel, Leicester."

Fucking hell. Not only was the invite to the wedding of Lila Holmes, but it was at work. Could it get any worse?

Yes.

"This invitation is for you, plus one guest."

Plus one.

I couldn't go alone; I'd never live it down.

I couldn't take anyone from work; it'd be weird and people would talk.

Maybe I could get off my arse and meet someone?

As I lay on my bed, checking my bedside clock every few minutes in the hope that hours had passed by, all I could see was Lila Holmes walking down the aisle with someone who looked exactly like me. They bounced merrily down the church steps in slow motion, as the friends and family of the happy couple covered them in pink and white confetti.

I repeated the same scenario until my alarm went off seven hours later. My eyes felt like they had sand under the lids, and every muscle in my body ached from a lack of sleep. If news of Lila's wedding wasn't a big enough dump on my day, I still had to speak to Jim and Sean about it too, which was always going to be fun.

I decided to wake myself up first, which meant jumping into a freezing cold shower. After the initial shock and shrinking of the nether regions, I closed my eyes and allowed the water to thud against my face. All I could see when I closed my eyes was a happy Lila Holmes bursting out of a church in a wedding dress.

I dried myself off, put on my suit, and headed downstairs to inform Sean and Jim of the wedding. I made myself a coffee and bowl of Shreddies and plonked myself down at the kitchen table, and stared glumly at the poorly painted white wall of our house.

Sean entered the kitchen first, wearing a pink fluffy dressing gown that his girlfriend has bought him as a joke, but now practically lived in. It made him look like an extra from the club scenes in *Scarface*, but you got used to it after a while.

"Morning buddy," he said, helping himself to coffee and Shreddies.

"Hey," I replied.

"What's up with you? Your eyes are bloodshot. Did you have a Wankathon last night?"

"Didn't sleep well."

"I'm surprised you slept at all with Jim entertaining."

"I've learned to shut that out of my mind. This was because of that invite."

I figured that it was better to just come out and tell him, rather than beat around the bush.

"Invite? Oh, you mean that fancy envelope? What was it?"

Before I could say anything, Jim burst in wearing his full army uniform.

"Morning, cunts!" Jim said, with a level of enthusiasm in his voice only proud parents can normally muster.

"Morning buddy," Sean replied.

When I didn't reply, Jim put his hands on my shoulders and squeezed them, causing me to go rigid and drop my cereal spoon in pain. No wonder he needs to butter those girls up with animated films, I thought. With a grip like that I'm surprised he hadn't killed someone, or torn his own cock off.

"What's up with you, sappy tits?" Jim asked.

"He got an invite last night. Didn't sleep."

Thanks, Sean.

"Yeah? Who was it from?"

I was too tired, fed up and sore from Jim's wank grip to try and change the subject or sidestep the issue altogether. I decided to blurt it out and see how my two best friends in the world would react.

"Lila Holmes," I said.

Sean's face dropped like a stone.

Jim fucked off.

The fact that Jim left a steaming cup of tea with the bag still in it told you everything you need to know about him. He didn't do what he called "the soppy stuff". Emotional support for Jim was saved for his work colleagues, which was fine, as they were facing death. Having a wobbly because you'd been invited to a wedding probably wasn't classed a valid threat at MI5.

At least I had Sean for support.

"I wonder if she's still fit."

Good start.

"I doubt she would have changed much," I replied.

Sean was staring into the middle-distance at this point.

"You're right. She was petite, wasn't she? 5'3", about eight stone?"

"This is making you sound really creepy, you know that, right?"

"I'm a coach. I need to know this stuff."

"For when you're choosing victims to fit in your van?"

"Hey, if you don't want my support…"

Sean put his coffee cup down and stood up to leave. In a moment of weakness, I lunged forward and grabbed his furry pink arm. Not a euphemism.

"I'm sorry buddy, I just don't know what to make of this. I'm all over the place."

Sean pulled out a chair and sat down next to me.

"What have you arrived at so far?" He asked.

"I keep seeing Lila Holmes walking out a church with a guy who looks like me, and I can't figure out why. I haven't thought about her in years, so it's not like I'm jealous or anything. It's weird."

"Maybe it's more that she's the last person you felt that way about, and now she's getting married. It's making you think that you're behind in that respect."

"Maybe."

"Either way, I really need a poo."

Suddenly my Shreddies didn't seem as inviting.

As Sean wandered off and left me to my thoughts, I started thinking about what he'd said, and it made sense. Lila was the dream girl, and because work had eaten up the majority of my time, I hadn't yet found a replacement.

That said, it was a shock to the system to discover that she had met, dated, got engaged to, and now was ready to walk down the aisle and spend the rest of her life with, someone else. Whereas I was just coming to terms with the idea of speaking to a member of the opposite sex again. That put me at least five years behind everyone else as far as I was concerned.

I chose to walk to work that day. By bike, the journey took 15 minutes, but I needed the extra time to think about things. I started replaying moments from my past in my head, like scenes from a movie. This movie was called "Jason Chapman Fucks It Up with Lila Holmes", and it was a teen sex comedy without any sex, but plenty of indie music and bad haircuts.

During my college years, it wasn't just Leisure and Tourism I studied badly. I also studied how not to get a girlfriend, and Lila Holmes was my unofficial course leader. She was also beautiful. I was infatuated with her from the moment she walked into the library and let out a huge laugh, and she was promptly told off by the librarian.

I had turned round to see what the commotion was all about (which was weird because I think I spent about 20 minutes in the library over the course of two years) and I saw her for the first time. She was biting her lip and miming "Sorry" to the librarian as she wandered in, and I just stared at her with my mouth wide open, like a moron. Her friend noticed and said something along the lines of "If you don't close your mouth you'll dribble" and I made a noise like Gregory Peck in *Captain Horatio Hornblower R.N.*

Lila was the kind of girl that turned heads and melted hearts. She was tiny in stature and had boundless energy. She would talk for hours and hours about anything but never outstay her welcome, and had a good word to say about everyone and everything. I've always been a cynical old codger at heart, but being around Lila made me feel like a kid. She brought the good out in people.

When we first started college, she had shoulder length brown hair. Then one day, she turned up with short cropped hair, similar to when Posh Spice first met David Beckham. This was back when hardly anybody had short hair, and it made her stand out even more. I would follow her around like Wile E. Coyote and Roadrunner, only I didn't want to eat her.

I still ended up falling off a cliff though.

There was a pub next to the college called The Station, which made a lot of money from underage drinking and therefore became the stomping ground of many smooth-faced kids who were still perfecting their deeper voices but wanted to get a beer after college.

One day, Lila was at The Station with two of her friends, and I remember watching her drinking a pint with two hands, which was the most adorable thing I had ever seen. Sean and I were playing pool at the table behind them, and for the first time in my life, I grew big enough balls to talk to a girl I had never met.

"If one you of ladies can beat me at pool, I'll buy you all a drink," I said.

Lila and her two friends turned round and smiled at me, and my butt cheeks clenched in pure unadulterated fear.

"You're on," Lila said.

I was in the unofficial Top Ten World's Worst Pool Players, but I still managed to destroy Lila with five balls to go. Then I realised that beating her so fast and easy wasn't going to keep her around much longer.

Twat.

Lila went to sit back with her friends, and sensing that my opportunity was fading fast, I blurted out the second coolest thing I'd ever said in my life.

"How about we meet in the middle and I only buy you a drink?"

Lila turned to her friends, who were sniggering amongst themselves, and then back to me. She nodded her approval and smiled. It took every ounce of strength in my body not to jump and punch the air or start dancing. Instead, I coolly walked to the bar and ordered two pints.

"Got any ID, mate?"

You motherfucker.

Lila appeared at my side.

"You already served us once, mate," Lila said, pointing to the half-finished evidence scattered on the table where her friends were seated.

Three cool things in a row was too much to ask for, but nevertheless, the guy reluctantly poured the beers.

Lila and I sat and chatted for two hours about our likes, dislikes, families, upbringings and the utter pointlessness of going to college to study Leisure and Tourism or Art, which she was studying.

I would have given anything to have spent the next two years locked in that moment, but like everything else in my life, I managed to fuck it up. After a month of flirting and telling everyone but her that I wanted to be her boyfriend, we finally plucked up the courage to make it official, at the Valentine's Day college social, which took place a few months before the summer holidays.

I remember that summer like guys in their forties remember the summer of 1990. It was hot, the music was great, and I didn't give a flying fuck about anything but Lila and my mates. At the time it was fantastic, but it was inevitable that it wouldn't last. We were far too young to be getting serious, but being the idiot that I am, I had a naïve plan that we would finish college, move in together and spend the rest of our days like the day we sat in The Station with those two pints.

We were together for a little over three months, and then it got weird. I was too needy, and Lila was sweet and popular, which meant that every time I saw her speaking to another guy, my lack of confidence would take over and I would convince myself that she was going to leave me for him. As far as I was concerned, I was punching far and beyond my weight division, and I didn't deserve a girl like Lila. I systematically fucked everything up as a result.

One day, I decided that I would 'test' her to see how much she liked me.

Bad idea.

The genius test was to split up with her, to see if she would fall to her knees and beg me to take her back. I remember saying something along the lines of, "You always seem more interested in everyone else, so I think we should see other people". Her response? "I don't want to see other people, but I only want to see you when you've grown up."

It was a great comeback, and no less than I deserved for playing games. If somebody as beautiful, smart and intelligent as Lila said that to me now, I'd say, "You're right, I'm a fucking idiot" and fight for them. But what did I do? Listened to The Smiths for two hours and bitched about Lila to my friends instead. What an absolute whopper.

The next nine months were really strange.

We clearly liked each other still, even though we made pathetic attempts to find other people, and we'd take snide pot shots at each other whenever possible. We must have been unbearable to be around for our friends. We were two emotionally immature people, too young to be in love and unsure of know how to deal with it.

Nine months after we had first split up, Lila and I found ourselves walking out of college together for some reason, and we hit it off again. By the time we'd walked into town, we were back together. It was the strangest ending to a rom-com ever.

"I was thinking… I clearly still like you… as you know… and… Fuck, I hope I've got this right. You still like me? What do you think about giving this another go?"

"Sure."

Cue Coldplay, rain and a kiss in the middle of the road.

It was never the same though. I liken it to how it must have been when The Stone Roses went back into the studio to record *The Second Coming*. The love was still there, but the momentum and the magic was lost. The split was inevitable.

It's hard to look at someone you absolutely adore, yet know that there is no way it's going to work. It's even worse when you have no idea why. But the relationship fizzled out yet again.

We split up for the final time on the last day of college, and it would be the last time I saw Lila Holmes in the flesh. I had to make a decision: try and make this work like we did over that first amazing summer, or give up now and walk away. I opted for the latter.

We met at the college gates. Lila was smiling and I was pacing.

"What's wrong?" she asked.

"Nothing… I've been thinking," I replied.

"That sounds ominous…"

"Is this going to work? Y'know, me and you… over the summer?"

This was followed by the longest pause in the history of mankind. I could practically hear the sinking of her heart through her clothes.

"I don't know," she said. "Don't you want to see what happens?"

"It's been a little 'off' for a while now, hasn't it?"

"My step-dad's been a dick. I'm sorry."

That was the point where an emotionally mature person would have understood the issue and focussed on supporting Lila, but I wasn't that person. All I was thinking was "How does that affect me?" and it was wrong on so many levels. I had the main reason for the troubles right in front of me, and I completely missed it.

"That's OK."

It was the "That's OK," that killed the Lila and Jason saga stone dead. I think she realised in that moment that – as much as it would hurt – it was time to cut me loose. I was thinking the same thing, just with a completely different view. I thought relationships were meant to be easy if you were in love, and this was hard. So it had to go.

"I'll see you around then?" I said.

"I hope so," Lila replied.

I leant forward and kissed her three times: Once on the forehead and once on each cheek, before holding her close to me. After a few seconds, Lila broke away from me and left the college gates, never stopping to look back. I watched her until she took the next corner, then looked down at the ground and tried my hardest not to be sick.

4. The Invite

I entered the hotel via the back entrance, through the door next to the beer keg cellar where the chefs went to smoke without being detected by the top brass. It was also the scene of one of Craig's legendary drunken flings, but it was hard to find a room other than the fifth conference room that Craig hadn't defiled, which meant that you were always careful where you put your hands. Fortunately, the staff fought to keep the hotel spotless.

I headed to the front desk to collect the DM keys and my walkie talkie, and the second Nicky on the front desk handed them over, a shaven-headed fat guy in an overly tight polo shirt turned to me and asked me the question that I dread to hear every time I come to work:

"Are you the manager?"

"No. I'm wearing a suit and have a massive badge saying 'Jason Chapman – Duty Manager' on my tit because I'm an Oscar-winning method actor playing a repressed and lonely twenty-something wanker in my next film. Now fuck off and die."

I didn't really say that, but I wanted to. "Yes. How can I help?" I said.

Like any great actor, you have to be able to put a face on and conduct yourself like a professional until the Grolsch poured and you could let the four letter words spill out.

With these 'angry guest' types, there were only ever three scenarios you had to deal with:

1) The customer was querying their final room bill (90% of cases their fault, 10% Craig's)

2) The customer had an issue with the staff, because a) The staff member was being treated like dirt and let the guard slip, or b) The member of staff hated your fucking guts and weren't afraid of letting you know about it, or c) The staff member was crap at their job

3) The toilet was broken or the shower didn't work

This particular angry guest fell into the first category, and wasn't prepared to pay for £45 worth of spirits and nuts from his minibar that he was saying he hadn't touched.

"Sir, these things happen," I said, calming the fat moose down a little. "These things happen all the time. Everything in the minibar have sensors fitted, and if they are moved, they are automatically added to your bill. I'll go up to the room and check to see if they've been taken or moved, and we'll get you checked out in no time."

Some customers expect to puff their chests out and act like a dick and have everything handed to them. Craig had taught me a valuable lesson: the customer is always right, unless they're fucking wrong.

I left the guest at the reception desk while I went up to the room to 'investigate'. Lo and behold, the fridge was emptied of its contents, and the bin was filled with empty spirit bottles and nut packets. Hardly a case for Poirot, but at least I got to make a fat meathead look a dickhead in front of the reception staff. Take that, Hercule.

When I came back to the reception desk, I was met with two grinning reception girls and no fatty.

"As soon as you stepped in the lift, the guest got agitated, paid the bill and left," said Nicky, trying hard not to high-five me.

"Bless him," I replied.

"He did tell me to tell you to go fuck yourself."

"Aww, did he fill out a comments card?"

I headed to the bar for my morning espresso and chin-wag with Jane. I had one aim: to do as little work as possible so I could sit in the housekeepers' office and watch films all day, whilst working out exactly what I was going to do about Lila and the wedding.

The walk home was a little different to the one to work that morning. For a start, I had watched two god-awful films back-to-back in the housekeeping office, one of which was some M. Shite Shamalamalamalam film, which Joe, an eighteen-year-old Maintenance trainee, thought was the greatest film known to man.

"M. Night Shyamalan is the new Jean Claude Van Goddard," he said, with the enthusiasm that only a clueless kid can possess.

On the walk home, I thought about Lila, only this time with a much clearer head than this morning. Instead of seeing her with a guy who looked like me, I saw her with Joaquin Phoenix, although that might have been because of the film I'd watched earlier. I had a much clearer vision now. Lila Holmes was getting married, and I really wanted to go to the wedding. She had thought of me whilst filling out her invites, and tracked my address down via a mutual friend, because we hadn't spoken for five years.

This meant that she had made an effort for me.

She must have thought about me.

She wanted me to come to the wedding.

She wanted to see me one last time.

I might have been overthinking this a little.

As I approached the house, I thought more about the college days and how our relationship ended. I was beginning to think that this was all about *closure*. She wanted a proper goodbye, and who was I to turn her down?

Entering the house, I could hear the sound of explosions and guns firing. Jim wasn't bringing his work home with him, he was simply watching *Predator* with Sean. They were sitting on the sofa, with Jim bouncing in his seat with glee as muscle-bound actors destroyed a rainforest in the name of entertainment.

I stood behind the sofa and watched the film for a few moments, looking down at Jim and Sean's contrasting views of Arnie and the gang's anti-Greenpeace campaign and wondering how I ever ended up living with two such completely different people.

"Are Bill Duke and Jesse Ventura a couple in real life?" I said, knowing that Jim would instantly rise to the bait.

"What? Don't be ridiculous," Jim replied, frowning.

"Oh yeah, I forgot that army guys are oblivious to the homoerotic overtones flowing through these macho films."

"Says the guy who spends an hour in the bathroom every morning."

"Hey Sean, has Jim cried yet?" I asked.

"He ain't got time to cry!" Sean quipped.

"Fuck you both," said Jim, his dummy flying across the room and hitting the TV.

Jim turned round and looked me up and down.

"You look better now," he said.

"Thanks? I'm not sure if this is a compliment or not."

"It is. Oh, and I'm sorry I bailed on you this morning. You know me, I'm shit with all that shit."

"That's a lot of shit. It's okay, anyway."

"Did you tear up the RSVP?" Jim asked.

"No," I said.

"When is the wedding?"

"Three months."

"Cool. Are you going?"

"Yeah."

"Bad idea."

"Why?" I asked.

"Because you're one big floppy cock who's been out of the game a long time. You want to turn up at that wedding having been at the top of your game for years or not at all. Lila's going to take one look at you and know that you've done nothing since splitting up with her, which will make her think a) You're gay, b) A weirdo, or c) Both."

"Thanks for your wise insights man, but I don't think Lila thinks like that."

"No? It's been five years since you last saw her. She could have been through anything during that time. The coked-up whore years, the boozy shag-hound days…"

"Do you have any examples of possible scenarios that don't begin with drugs and drink and end with excessive shagging?"

"No."

"Brilliant."

Sean attempted to steer the conversation back into the realm of reality.

"I'm with you on this one, buddy. Lila doesn't strike me as the kind of girl who would fuck around. It's more likely that she met this guy after you and that's it. And she wasn't a judgemental person at all. If she's invited you, it's because she wants to see you again. It's called 'ticking boxes'. Weddings work like that."

"Really?"

"Yeah."

Jim much preferred it when he was talking. It involved more sex and alcohol, and less of what he perceived to be whining. He screwed his face up like a wasp had just stung his nutsack, and prepared to fight back.

"You two really don't understand women, do you? Lila Holmes is inviting you to this wedding to show you what you're missing. Make no mistake about it. And you're playing right into her hands by turning up off your game."

"I think you're talking rubbish." I hit back.

"Yeah? Then why aren't we invited then?"

He had a point. But before I could think of something to counter with that was better than 'fuck off', Sean raised his hand.

"I've been invited," he said.

This changed things. If Lila had invited Sean, that played into the 'ticking boxes' theory. But at the same time, it also dispelled my theory that she was thinking about me and invited me for reasons other than simply making up the numbers.

"It came this morning," Sean continued. "I'm only going to go if you are, obviously."

Let me just pull my heart out of my arse and let you know, mate...

"Sure. We should go."

Jim, feeling a little left out, turned the volume up on *Predator*. Arnie and the gang were still firing into the rainforest, and in that moment, I wouldn't have minded being stood in front of them.

I headed to the kitchen to make myself the perfect 'I've just been kicked in the balls' sandwich: two slices of large white Warburton's Toastie bread, with crunchy peanut butter and salt and vinegar crisps. Plenty of sat-fats, salt and crunch. Just what I needed.

Sean followed me into the kitchen and made himself a coffee out of the monstrosity of an espresso machine he had just bought, which looked like it could send Kyle Reese back to 1984. Sean loved his gadgets. He was the first person I knew who had a George Foreman grill, and he bought a DVD player from the United States for $1000 before DVD's became the norm. It looked amazing, but wasn't much cop when you had no DVD's to play on it.

"Do you want to go to the wedding?" he asked.

"I don't know. It's weird. When I got up this morning I felt awful about it. Like the world had passed me by, y'know? Then I convinced myself that this was about closure. But now I know you've been invited too… It's made me realise my place in her life."

Sean looked down at his coffee and sighed. He knew what it was like to be a huge part of someone's life and then lose them.

"If I can be honest with you, I think you need this," he said. "You need to know whether your current situation is because you haven't got over her, or because she's become the measuring stick that all others have to be judged by."

"I think you're right."

Jim entered the kitchen and grabbed a beer from the fridge.

"What are you two talking about?" he asked.

"The wedding," Sean replied.

"I'm a little annoyed that I haven't been invited. Can I be your plus one, Sean? I don't want to miss Ennis crying into a piece of wedding cake. It'll be hilarious."

"Can you fuck off please, you're not helping with this," I said.

Jim was not the most sensitive of people, but at the same time, he was also quite needy in that he didn't like to be left out of the loop, even if his advice to 99.9% of issues would be 'fuck them', 'fuck her' or 'go fuck yourself', so you could imagine what me saying 'You're not helping with this' would lead to.

"Oh, I'm sorry, I have testosterone flowing through my veins and not the greatest hits of Morrissey. I do apologise. I'll be watching Arnold Schwarzenegger fight a space alien if anyone wants me. Assholes."

Jim stormed out of the kitchen. It was in moments like this that I feared for the safety of every single person in the British Army.

Sean just shook his head and necked the rest of his coffee.

"Shall we go back in there?" he asked.

"Yeah, I guess so."

I grabbed my sandwich and headed back to the living room. Crisps were breaking up and falling on the carpet as I attempted to eat my sandwich whilst walking, but I didn't care because hoovering was Jim's job, and he was being a cock. It was my job to clean the kitchen and the bathroom, and Sean's to do the gardening, polishing and any handyman jobs around the house. As a former homeowner, he felt a little superior to us in the house stakes, due to his knowledge of fuse boxes and the fact that he gave a shit.

If I couldn't turn it off and back on again and get the desired result, I would kick it and walk away, or pour a glass of whisky into it in an attempt to be as cool as Kurt Russell.

Sean and I sat either side of Jim on the sofa, and watched as Arnie ran around the jungle caked in mud and monkey shit, accompanied by Alan Silvestri's epic film score.

"What conclusion did you come to then?" Jim asked from back in his pram.

"Arnie wins in the end. Greenpeace loses," I joked.

Jim ignored me and turned to Sean for a proper answer.

"We're going to the wedding," Sean said.

"I'm very happy for you."

"Do you want to be my plus one?" Sean asked.

Jim's eyes lit up like a Christmas tree. I'm not sure if it was because he'd been included, or because he'd pictured himself arriving at the wedding reception in his full army uniform, and all the shagging that he imagined that would lead to.

"Are you kidding? I'd love to go," he said. "I can witness this clown having his heart broken in real time!"

At any other time in the history of our friendship, I would have laughed this off or given Jim a dead arm for his troubles. But the lack of sleep, the fact that it was Lila, and the two hours of my life I had wasted that day watching an M. Night film had eroded my tolerance to twattiness. I launched out of my seat and stood of the way of the TV, therefore guaranteeing myself Jim's full attention.

"D'ya know what, mate? Sometimes you can be a complete prick."

"You know what to expect of me. Don't act so surprised," Jim said.

"As if that justifies having no regard for your friend's feelings," I said.

Still nothing, and Jim was in full dick-mode now, mainly because I was standing between him and his daily dose of Arnie.

"You're twenty-three years of age and you're still pining over someone you cocked it up with five years ago. You haven't even seen her in that time, so how on earth do you expect to deal with actually being in the same room with her, when she's necking some twat she's just married and wearing a wedding dress? You'll shit your pants. I'm trying to make you see sense by giving you a bit of stick, and you're getting out of your pram, which just highlights how unprepared for this you really are."

Had I not changed at all in five years? Was I still wet behind the ears when it came to love? Whatever the answer, Jim had knocked the wind out of me, and I felt worse than ever.

Sean tried to keep the peace as I sank into the giant bean bag next to the TV.

"Now-now children, let's call calm down. Hey Jason, do you remember those songs you wrote about Lila at college?"

Sean and I had written series of songs together as seventeen-year-old love-sick puppies. The only problem was that neither of us could play a musical instrument, or sing, or had a musical bone in our body. What actually happened was that we wrote poems, but we thought that if we told people we wrote poems, we'd look like twats. Saying that we wrote songs was much cooler, even if our songs were some of the worst ever written.

Nevertheless, it broke the mood quite nicely, and brought a smile to my face.

"The classic: 'I Love You (Almost as Much as I Want to Kill You)'"

"Very eighties Manchester," Jim chimed in.

"We were listening to a lot of The Smiths back then, and Badly Drawn Boy…"

"Badly Written Songs," Jim was adamant that he was going to destroy the mood. "And they say romance is dead. It's just laid dormant in your tiny flaccid cocks. I'm glad I was away during your college years. I would never have gotten laid if I'd been around you two."

"The majority of yours were your bunk buddies though mate," Sean said, bringing the smile back to my face at Jim's expense.

"Lap it up. But wherever I go in the world, I get women, and the reason for that is that I have confidence and I don't write songs about girls that I'm scared to talk to. I wouldn't be able to write a song if I was in a band, because I'd be too busy shagging until my cock fell off, which would then become the name of my solo album."

You had to hand it to Jim, when he jumped onto his high horse and started ranting, there was no stopping him. He turned his attention to Sean.

"I am everything you Morrissey-wannabes want to be. How many girls have you slept with, Sean?"

"Five. It would have been six but your dad came home."

"Dick."

I should've known not to laugh, because it meant that Jim honed in on me.

"Look mate, I don't mean to be a dick, but what you're doing isn't healthy. You've got to move on with your life, mate. The best place to start is to stop thinking and start fucking. Let the blood flow from your brain down to your main vein, and *then* you can turn up at the wedding, say hello and goodbye, then move on to pastures new. Boom."

Silence. Except for the sound of Arnie roaring from the top of a tree like a drunk Tarzan. Jim was right on every level, but I still wanted to lose my shoe in his face.

"I think you're right."

"I think so too," Jim replied.

"But I'm not like you, I can't fuck a different girl to 'Cats and Dogs' every night. Which is really weird, by the way."

"And that's why Lila's marrying someone else and not you."

The sucker punch. Down goes the champ. He tries desperately to get up, but he can't beat the referees count to ten, and he's out. Defeated.

Sean could see that I was hurt by Jim's remark, but he also knew that he couldn't win here. The rule of three: If you stick up for one side more than the other, the other person will hate your guts. But sitting on the fence doesn't help any of you either.

"Mate, that was a little harsh," he said.

Jim sat back in his chair and folded his arms. I just stared at him, waiting for an apology that was never going to come. The next time Jim opened his mouth to speak, it needed to be about anything but Lila, or at least something nice, or we were done.

Not Jim's style.

"You guys are very philosophical, but at the end of the day, you've seen less vagina than a blind gynaecologist. And now Lila's marrying some turd because instead of giving her reasons to leave, he's given her an eight inch reason to stay, something you never did. I like this guy. I think we're going to get on well."

Jim finished saying his piece, and couldn't look at me. He knew that he'd gone too far.

I stood up, gave him the middle finger, and got the fuck out of there before I blew my top. Sean knew that he was the only one who could defuse the situation, and he followed me out the room and into the hallway.

"Don't listen to him, mate. He's only spitting his dummy out because he didn't get an invite. You know he gets weird when we talk about the college days. You know as well as I do that he's jealous he wasn't around for it."

"I know. I guess I just wasn't in the mood for listening to the truth. Goodnight, man."

"Bollocks to goodnight. Let's go for a beer, you can talk my ear off about all of that soppy shit."

Beer with Sean or a night staring up at the ceiling thinking about Lila? Easy decision.

The pub around the corner from our house was called The Rose Garden, but it might as well have been called Don't Look Up, because making eye contact with any of the toothless wonders who drank in there was never a good idea. They'd smash a bottle over your head rather than talk to you, but the beer was cheap, so for us, it was a risk worth taking. The place stank of stale beer and the tables were stickier than a fourteen-year-old's duvet cover, but it had a certain charm.

"I never understand why pubs like this have a playground out the back. Who in their right mind would bring a kid in here, unless they were swapping it for some crack?"

Sean had a very good point. Surely most people went to the pub to escape their kids, not get pissed whilst they played on the swings? Baffling.

"Right. You have my ears, and you have a pint of lukewarm fake-Aussie piss. Go!"

Sean had always been the voice of reason in my life, and a great sounding board for when I need to talk about the kind of things that Jim shied away from: Love, relationships and all of the good stuff.

"Are we really going to go?" I asked.

"Why shouldn't we? We'll have a good time and you'll get the closure you need. After what I've just witnessed, you definitely need it."

"It's weird. It's all I can think about. It's made me realise that I don't have anything of note filling the gaps between her walking away and me sitting in this boozer."

"It's a hard lesson to learn. Jim's right though. You've got the opportunity to use this wedding as a launch-pad to the next phase of your life."

"It is going to be hard to watch her dance around with some twat, knowing that if I'd made an effort, it could've been me. I mean, I made no effort at all to keep her with me. I let her go. And in the five years that have followed, I've had three one-night stands and two relationships that felt more like a jail sentence. Not one second of any of those experiences measure up to one second that I spent in her company…"

I noticed that Sean was looking rather nervously over my shoulder, and had not been listening to me at all.

"Are you listening to me?" I asked.

"Yes mate, and I can honestly tell you that the wedding is going to be the most important goodbye after this one."

Sean necked his pint in less than three gulps. It would have been impressive, if it wasn't so weird.

"What are you talking about? What's wrong with you?"

"I've been eye-fucking this girl since we got here, and she's just been joined by her boyfriend, who's built like a brick shithouse."

Knowing the kind of clientele that The Rose Garden entertained on a daily basis, I grabbed my pint and attempted to down it. It took me five gulps, and I followed up with a Barney from *The Simpsons* burp that almost blew Sean over.

What a couple of classy bastards.

We dashed for the exit and headed off into the night and back home, where Jim would most likely be doing angry sit-ups or hoovering like Mrs Doubtfire on crack.

I felt a little better, but another poor night's sleep was looming, which meant that my weekend was going to be horrific. The hotel would be filled with 300-400 people a night at the weekend, with the majority of them being families or drunks.

They were just as annoying as each other.

Jim had made a last minute booty call and was entertaining to *Lilo and Stitch* that night. Another kid's film permanently ruined for me. I often wondered how girls ever fell for his shtick. But I didn't *really* want to know.

I was thinking about it too much, but anything was better than thinking about Lila, as I would need to sleep at some point. I closed my eyes and tried to think about something other than Lila, work, or the sound of Jim and his date having a really intense orgasm.

Fuck my life.

5. Pictures of Lila

3:04am.

Perfect time for a bit of nostalgia.

I was thinking about the night Lila and I got together. It was a night I could recall on an analyst's couch any time. The memory was right there in Technicolor. I hadn't thought about it in a while, but as soon as I went there, it all came flooding back, like finding an old VHS tape with your favourite films on it from when you were 9 years old.

The social was an end-of-term party that was held at a nightclub just outside of town called Holdens, which was the kind of place that made you feel like you were a cool adult when you were an underage drinker, but the older you got, the more you realised that it wasn't a nightclub at all, just a large bar with a loud speaker and shiny dancefloor. It was a good craic for a seventeen-year-old whose only experience of drinking was paying the local weirdo an extra couple of quid to get us booze from the local Unwins.

There were three socials every year: the Xmas social, the Valentine's social and the end of the year social. The Xmas one was a little cliquey because nobody knew each other outside of their own circles yet. The Valentine's social was a snogfest, and the end of year social was a little emotional, as people were leaving for university, and the boarding house students were heading back to Botswana, Dubai or Germany.

At the Xmas social, Sean, an old friend from primary School called Tom and I arrived suited and booted and stiffly shuffled around the club looking awkward, drinking bottles of Smirnoff Ice because we thought that's what cool clubbers drank. It was alcoholic sugar, and the rush gave me flushed cheeks that made me look like Adam Ant.

We sat at a round table all night, bopping our heads in an attempt to blend in – we hated club music with a passion as we were Britpop kids – and spent most of the night staring at the girls we fancied but hadn't grown the courage to talk to yet. If Jim had been there, he would have been our way in, but he was learning how to kill people in his 18 month army induction at this point.

The socials were legendary for somebody being absolutely trashed, and often for the first time in their lives. There was a kid called Andy who had never drank before, yet drank five cans of extra strength lager – the kind only homeless people drink – and proceeded to dance with his shirt off on the dancefloor until he projectile vomited like Regan from *The Exorcist*, still dancing in circles as it flowed out of him and showering everyone in regurgitated lager and canteen food as he went for glory.

At the end of the night, Andy was found lying on his back in a gutter on the main street, which unfortunately for him was downhill from the top of the road, a perfect spot for a cheeky piss before going home. He was snoring away merrily, unaware that the biggest stream of concentrated piss was coming right for him like the *Mission: Impossible* fuse burning down. Fortunately for Andy, somebody noticed and pulled him out of the firing line. I never saw him drunk again.

We poured out of the club at the end of the night and climbed onto one of three buses marked for each of the three most local towns. The college supplied them for their beloved students, and they filled up with people who were either getting off with each other, sleeping or fighting.

If you were lucky, you got to be in the first camp. The second camp either resulted in someone farting in your face, putting make-up on you or taking a photo of you for publication in the student newspaper or on the college noticeboard.

If the first social was a learning curve, the second one, Valentine's, was the graduation. By this point, Lila and I had met at the pub, bonded, flirted and all the other stuff, but failed to turn that into anything resembling a relationship, or so much as a cheeky kiss. At school I had 'been out' with almost every girl in my year, but at college, everyone was talking about 'seeing' each other. *"Are you going out with [Insert Name]?" "Nah mate, I'm just seeing her."*

What the fuck did that mean?

I assumed that 'seeing' was what everyone was doing, and as much as I wanted Lila as a girlfriend, I didn't want to embarrass myself by asking her out and finding out she only wanted to 'see' me.

Damon Albarn once sang: "Love in the Nineties is paranoid".

He wasn't wrong. I needed an instruction manual.

In the lead-up to the social, all the people on my course were asking if I was going to get with Lila, and I'm sure people were saying the same to her about me. The problem was, nobody was communicating this information back to me. At school, we would just say "Ask so-and-so out for me" and the next thing you knew, you had a girlfriend. Didn't work that way at college. You had to man-up and do it yourself, which wasn't my speciality.

Lila and I flirted around the subject whenever we saw each other, asking each other questions like, "Are you going to the Valentine's social?" "Yeah? Any Valentine's in mind?" "Maybe huh? That's interesting."

Ask her, you cock!

On the night of the social, Sean and Tom came over to my house, disappeared into my bedroom and drank eight cans of Fosters each whilst listening to The Complete Stone Roses on repeat. The trajectory of those wistful two hours in the run up to catching the bus to the social went something like this:

1. "So Young" – 3:30 – Sitting on the bed thinking about Lila.

2. "Tell Me" – 3:50 – Discussing how it took The Stone Roses five years to make the first album, then another five years to make the second.

3. "Sally Cinnamon" (7" remix version) – 2:50 – Dancing.

4. "Here It Comes" – 2:40 – The "Do you think Lila likes me?" conversation.

5. "All Across the Sands" – 2:40 – Sean sings along with his eyes closed.

6. "Elephant Stone" (7" version) – 3:00 – We all stand up and dance. Dad shouts "Shut up" and we fall about laughing.

7. "Full Fathom Five" – 3:18 – Pranging out over whether we'll get served tonight. Tom asks "What is this backwards music shit?"

8. "The Hardest Thing in the World" – 2:39 – The first time I'll ever say "This song reminds me of me and Lila". It won't be the last.

9. "Made of Stone" – 4:11 – We all close our eyes and sing along.

10. "Going Down" – 2:46 – Oasis and Stone Roses "Who has the best B-sides?" discussion.

11. "She Bangs the Drums" (7" edit version) – 3:42 – Lying on my back, singing along, thinking about how I'm going to play this one out with Lila.

12. "Mersey Paradise" - 2:44 - Sean goes full-on Liverpool supporter and sings along.

13. "Standing Here" - 5:05 - No one talks for five minutes and five seconds. Lots of drinking is done.

14. "I Wanna Be Adored" (7" edit version) - 3:28 - Sean utters "Tune" to break the ice. We discuss whether or not The Stone Roses is the best album of all time.

15. "Waterfall" (7" remix version) - 3:36 - Close your eyes and sing along time.

16. "I Am the Resurrection" (7" remix version) - 3:41 - We all break the seal and air-drum along to the greatest album closer ever.

17. "Where Angels Play" - 4:15 - Starting to get tipsy now. The confidence starts to grow. "Fuck it. I'm just going to say: 'Lila, you're a babe, I'm a babe. Let's make babies'." Everyone agrees that saying that would be a bad idea.

18. "Fools Gold" (7" version) - 4:15 - No one talks. We all mimic Reni's closed-eyes drumming from the video.

19. "What The World Is Waiting For" - 3:55 - Fuck you, Dad. We get up and start dancing again, this time throwing each other around the room.

20. "Something Burning" (7" version) - 3:37 - Getting our breath back during the slow grooves of SB.

21. "One Love" (7" version) – 3:40 – Quickly downing the last can so we can make the bus in time. We each take it in turns to use the bathroom again, and dad kicks us out of the house.

We wandered out into the street, dressed to kill in ill-fitting black suits, white shirts and black ties. We thought we looked awesome, whereas to the rest of the world we looked like young people trying to look older so they can get served alcohol. Either way, we had a newfound sense of confidence now due to the Stone Roses and Fosters.

As we strolled on down to get the bus from the college, my attentions turned towards Lila again. Sean and Tom would be happy enough just to talk to a girl, whereas my entire night hinged on Lila becoming my girlfriend.

No pressure.

"I think I'm going to buy her a drink, take her into a quiet area and talk to her," I said.

"That sounds like the inner monologue of a serial killer, but good luck to ya," Tom replied, as he failed miserably in his attempt to walk along the kerb.

"Seriously, do you think that's the right plan?"

"Definitely," Sean replied.

"Cool. I'll do that. Just gotta pick the right moment."

Looking back now, I'm amazed I have any experience with girls whatsoever. Who plans having a conversation with someone? How would that ever work? Especially after filling myself up with Fosters, which had gone right through me and had now turned my bladder into a ticking time bomb. My Granddad pissed less than this. By the time we came to the bus, we were all desperate for the bog again. Nothing screams 'cool' like three guys in suits bending at the knees and grimacing in pain.

We managed to get on the bus, which would have been the perfect opportunity to talk to Lila had she not lived in Stamford. It meant that our first conversation would have to be inside the club, and that meant shouting in her ear as 'Freed from Desire' blasted out of the speakers.

The bus took 40 minutes, and every second was spent going through every scenario that would end with Lila becoming my girlfriend. Most of these imaginings ended with us walking around hand-in-hand, kissing and cuddling like a scene from a Backstreet Boys video. The real-life version would probably be something like this:

"Will you go out with me?"

"Yes."

"Awesome."

We kiss.

Cue awkwardness.

"See ya!"

Walk away in opposite directions.

The bus pulled into Stamford and crowds of adolescent college kids walked towards the nightclub like moths to a blue light, only without the imminent doom of having your insides burnt out by electricity. I'd be praying for that if Lila turns me down. But she wouldn't do that, would she? She likes me, right?

I needed a drink.

Sean, Tom and I headed to the bar and proceeded to order two blue Aftershocks each. For starting drinks. Yeah. Good idea. If looking like pissed-up old men in suits at the bus stop wasn't uncool enough, screwing your face up and sticking your tongue out in horror when you've just necked an Aftershock might have taken home the award for the uncoolest moment ever.

"Here's to swimming with bowlegged women," Sean said, before downing his second shot.

I've never seen a man run to the toilet so fast.

I stood at the bar with Tom, looking around the room for signs that Lila was there. I couldn't see her or her friends, but it was early. Maybe she was planning on making me wait. A fashionably late entrance. Girls do that.

I ordered Smirnoff Ices for myself, Tom and the puke monster, who was returning to the bar looking pale and a little ashamed of himself. If any of us had stopped to think, we might have realised that drinking sugary drinks or shots of 40% mouthwash probably wasn't the best idea. But at that time, the only thing that mattered was being drunk enough to approach the opposite sex without sounding like Bill and Ben on smack.

"There's somebody doing coke off the toilet seat in there," said Sean.

"Really? And you saw it?" I replied.

"Yeah. I had to barge past him to puke in the toilet. The other one was occupied. He wasn't impressed."

"Off the toilet seat? I've never snorted sweat from someone's arse cheeks before, I bet that's lovely," said Tom, before necking half a Smirnoff Ice in one gulp.

As much as I could have talked about cocaine, arseholes and Sean's vomit all night, I had a mission to complete.

"I'm going to look for Lila," I said.

"Good luck!"

Sean and Tom gave me the thumbs up as I left, before falling back into their delightful conversation. They probably had the right idea. Here I was, walking through a nightclub I had no business being in, looking for a girl I was falling for yet had no plans for what I was going to say if I bumped into her.

It was at that moment, the record that changed my life started to play.

The song was 'Bizarre Love Triangle' by New Order. The 1994 London Records version. The moment it started to play, adrenaline shot up my spine, and I felt like I was home. New Order were one of my favourite bands, and hearing the song gave me the confidence I was lacking. I'd felt like a fake, that I didn't belong. Now I was comfortable. I mimed along with the words as I wandered through the crowds of people, my shoulders pinned back instead of slumped, and with a spring in my step. People nodded at me as I passed. I was cool, or at least I would be for the three minutes and fifty-four seconds the song lasted.

It was during Peter Hook's amazing bass solo that I saw her. I had walked from one end of the club to the other, and was making my way back to Tom and Sean, who were still drinking liquid diabetes at the bar.

Then suddenly, there she was…

She was wearing tight blue jeans and a plain white T-shirt, which was glowing in the UV light. She looked perfect as she danced along to the song. We caught each other's eye and I froze. Lila smiled and came running towards me from the dancefloor. She put her head on my shoulder and whispered "Dance with me," into my ear.

"I can't dance," I yelled into her ear.

"Who cares?" she replied.

Lila took my hands in hers and backed slowly towards the dancefloor. I felt like a complete idiot. Here was the true definition of 'free spirit' standing right in front of me, dressed cool and casual, and I looked like I was auditioning for Bugsy Malone.

I estimated that I had about 90 seconds before something a little more awful came on over the speakers and I would look even more of a fool, and for once in my life, I let myself go and went with it. I threw my cares to one side for the sake of being with Lila, safe in the knowledge that however badly I danced, as long as I didn't take my shirt off and vomit on everyone, I'd be just fine.

The final electronic drums came in, and the DJ lazily transitioned New Order to 'You Make Me Wanna' by Usher.

A slow jam. Now?

I stepped away from Lila a little, but she was having none of it. She pulled me to her and we slow danced throughout the entire song, without saying a word to each other. I'd spent all of that time worrying about what to say, and silence was saying everything for me. Cheers, Usher.

My date with Steph just went to show that I'd learned nothing from my teenage years. Drinking fast was not a good idea, especially when you're nervous or haven't eaten. I'd eaten nothing since breakfast, and the Aftershocks and the Fosters were now joining forces against me.

Usher was making a decision as to whether he was going to leave the one he was with to start a new relationship with someone else, and I started to feel lightheaded. At the end of this track, I had to take Lila into the quiet area to talk and – more importantly – sober up enough so as to avoid making a twat out of myself.

"I'm going to the bathroom. I'll see you out here in a minute?" Lila said.

"Cool," I replied, my eyes starting to glaze over.

Lila smiled at me before moving through the crowd towards the toilets, giving Sean and Tom a wave as she passed the bar. I made my way to the bar.

Sean and Tom were happy for me.

"Holy shitballs you are in with Lila!" Sean said.

"Mate, I'm so proud," said Tom.

"Thanks guys," I said. "But I'm in trouble. I can't see straight and I don't wanna fuck this up. What can I do?"

"Honestly? Throw up," Sean said. "I feel fan-fucking-tastic since spewing. It'll sort you right out."

I had few options left, and the lights of the club were starting to blur. My thoughts were becoming weird, too. I thought back to Andy lying in that gutter, and decided that touching the back of my throat with two fingers was the perfect Reset button.

"I'm going to puke," I said.

"Good idea. Have a mint."

Sean had thought of everything. He handed me a XXX mint and I went to the toilet. Before I could get to the door, a bouncer stood in my way.

"What's that you've got in your hand, mate?" he asked.

I lifted my hand up to his face and opened my palm to reveal a mint that I had no intention of snorting off the toilet seat.

"OK, you can go."

Phew.

As I approached the toilets, I dropped the mint at the door. Gutted, I thought, and almost fell over trying to catch it. I was going to have to throw up and get back to Sean for a second mint before bumping into Lila again. No problem. Just needed to go into the right toilet now. No way could I fuck that up.

I fucked that up.

I entered the ladies by mistake, which looked like the Overlook Hotel (without the dead twins, ghosts and crazy caretakers) compared to the men's toilets, which looked like the ones from *Trainspotting*. It took me a couple of seconds to realise that I had entered the wrong bathroom, but by then it was too late. It was like walking into another world, where everyone talked, put make-up on and hung out rather than puked and pissed on each other's shoes at the urinal.

Talking to her friend at the sinks was Lila. She spotted me right away and tried to usher me out the door, but Amy, a girl from my course, stepped in.

"You can't go back out there without someone checking to see if the bouncers there," she said. "If he sees you coming out of here he'll kick the crap out of you, whether it was innocent or not."

"Why did you come here?" asked Lila, which in my drunken state made me think of Suedehead.

Snap out of it, you twat.

"I wanted to talk to you," I said, deciding that the noble romantic approach was better than saying 'I dropped a mint and I'm a bit of a knob'.

"Quick, get in here!"

Lila pushed me into the end cubicle and locked the door.

"You're an idiot. If you get caught in here, you'll be kicked out."

"I don't care. I'm a bit drunk and I made a decision that was born out of…"

"What?" Lila asked.

"I dunno," I said.

Lila smiled and started giggling. There aren't many sights and sounds that pair up better.

"I've been thinking," I said.

"Are you okay? Do you need to sit down?"

Hearing the words 'sit down' reminded me that it might be a good idea judging by my level of drunkenness. I sat down on the toilet and looked up at Lila, who was standing with her arms folded at the cubicle door with a smirk on her face.

"I'm comfortable here. There's a nice smell, the music isn't too loud. I'm not going anywhere," I said.

"I don't think that's going to happen. Unless…"

Lila approached slowly. My heart pounded, and got to danger levels by the time she was close enough that I could feel her breath on my face. Do I stand and meet her? No, sitting on the toilet is much cooler. Stand, you fool!

My legs, my head and my heart were not on speaking terms at this moment.

I managed to stand just as Lila's lips touched mine for the first time. As my eyes closed, I saw that hers had closed too, and she pulled her body close to mine. She was toned, and it made me consider that if I could feel how toned she was, she would be able to feel how untoned I was. Why was I thinking negatively about myself whilst locking lips with the girl of my dreams?

She pulled away from the kiss first, and grabbed my ridiculous tie with both hands.

"I forgot to say that you look nice in your suit," she said.

"You look amazing in anything you wear," I replied.

Lila kissed me again, and suddenly I was as sober as a judge. The problem was, most judges don't have to manoeuvre their way out of ladies' toilets without being battered by a bouncer. I decided that now would be a perfect time to ask the big question.

"I… really like you, y'know," I said.

"I like you, too. But we haven't known each other that long."

"What? We know each other well enough."

"Did you know I have a tattoo?"

"I didn't know that was part of the initiation process."

"It's not, but it shows that we hardly know each other."

I had to think of something fast. Don't let the conversation take a negative turn.

"Can I see your tattoo?" I said.

"Not really."

"What is it?"

"It's the Chinese symbol for 'angel'. My parents still don't know about it."

"Rebel. So can I see it?"

"It's on my bum."

"Well now I have to see it."

Lila laughed and stepped away from me. She started to unbutton my jeans, and I counted along in my head as each button came undone. If I had been wearing a bow-tie, I would have started spinning. It was by far the hottest situation I had found myself in.

Her right hand pulled down on her unbuttoned jeans to reveal the buttock with the symbol on it. It was the cutest little thing I'd ever seen.

The tattoo, on the other hand, I barely noticed.

"Cute," I said.

Lila started to button her jeans back up.

"Thank you," she said.

"Now that I've seen that you're an angel, maybe we can move forward with this thing?"

"Are you serious?" she said.

"Of course."

"You don't want to just see each other?"

Again with the 'seeing' thing. If only Google had existed back then…

I couldn't believe that Lila was asking me that question. Like I had any other options, or would possibly want anyone else. But the fact that Lila asked me the question was revealing vulnerabilities that I knew were there, and had made me fall for her in the first place.

"I don't want to see you. I want to be your boyfriend. Full time. Serious. Old school."

Lila finished buttoning up her jeans and came back for another kiss.

"OK," she said.

Never had two letters coming together sounded so fucking magnificent. I wanted to jump up and down and scream "I have a girlfriend!" but I quickly realised that it would make me an absolute tit, so I opted for "Cool" instead, and stood grinning like an idiot with no idea what to say or do next.

"Let's get out of here before you get killed," Lila said.

Fortunately for me – and my teeth – the bouncer was nowhere to be seen, and Lila and a couple of other girls managed to sneak me back into the club unnoticed. Only this time, I was holding hands with my girlfriend.

I had a girlfriend.

I was at a nightclub with my fucking girlfriend.

Girlfriend.

Girlfriend.

Girlfriend.

The first place Lila and I visited as a couple was the bar, where Tom and Sean had collected a set of empty and sticky Aftershock glasses. When they saw us approaching hand-in-hand, they cheered like Robbie Fowler had scored at Anfield and was heading towards them for a celebratory embrace.

I didn't have another drink for the rest of the night, and I didn't look anywhere else but straight at Lila. When you're young and in love, you don't consider other people, or how they would perceive your blatant rudeness. All I could think about was where the next kiss was going to come from, and how beautiful Lila's tattooed bottom was.

At the end of the night, Lila grabbed her lift home and I got the bus home with an absolutely hammered Sean and a sobering Tom. Sean fell asleep on the bus and was snoring like a lion with his mouth wide open, and we held competitions as to who could throw things into his mouth from the furthest distance. A girl named Kerry managed to get a bullseye with a roll-up filter from 12 yards, which didn't even wake Sean up, despite the fact that it could have choked him to death.

"Tonight went pretty well, didn't it buddy?" Tom asked me as we drove home down a long, dark country road.

"It was perfect," I replied.

3:46am.

I was starting to think that nostalgia wasn't such a great idea after all.

6. The Voices of Reason

Going to work off the back of a shocking night's sleep had now become a regular occurrence, and I was not a fan. The hotel trade works in rises and falls: One minute you're swanning around doing nothing, and the next you've got a hundred and fifty businessmen checking in expecting to have their bags taken up to their rooms. I could deal with anything when I wasn't feeling like someone had taken a dump inside my head.

I headed to the bar for my espresso fix, and found Jane waiting for me with one already made, and a smirk on her face.

"What's so amusing?" I asked.

"Nothing, Panda Eyes," she replied.

"Don't tease me today, Jane. I'm very fragile."

"You seem to be fragile quite a lot at the minute. Are you not getting too much sleep? And if so, is that for good reasons or bad reasons?"

"Bad. Sadly."

"Wanna talk about it?"

I threw the espresso down my throat like it was a whisky, and I was running a saloon in a 1940s Western.

"I do, actually." I said.

"Is it girl problems? Who is she and what are you blaming her for?"

"Cheeky bugger! I've been invited to the wedding of my dream girl."

"That's got to hurt."

"Yeah, it does. And it's my own fault."

"Why?"

"Because I had my chance five years ago and I blew it."

"Five years ago… so you were six?" Jane sniggered at my expense. "It's called 'life experience', Jason. We have to suck it up, learn from it and move on," she said.

"I guess," I said.

The sound of Craig's shoes on the hotel's wooden floor made it impossible for him to make a surprise appearance.

"Aye-up Cunto," he said, arriving behind me.

"Hey," I said.

"Take a break, love."

"Cheers, Craig," Jane said, gently squeezing my arm in a quiet showing of support as she left to have a cigarette out the back.

"You seem edgy," I said.

"I had a fight with the Missus last night. I need everybody to wipe their own arse tonight or blood will be spilled."

"OK, Maximus. I have a clean arse, don't worry about me."

"I know I don't have to worry about you. Fucking Mike is on tonight though. I might have to be restrained so stay close to me. I told you about Christmas Day, right?"

Christmas Day was the one day of the year nobody wanted to work, regardless of whether you liked your family or had any religious affiliation. In the hotel trade, the majority of managers, supervisors and contracted staff got pulled into it. The casual staff would be on double time, but the only staff willing to do it were the uni students who couldn't be arsed to go home at Xmas. They would rather earn the extra cash and dodge the awkward questions their parents had waiting for them about their bank balance and alcohol intake.

"I heard something about it…"

"One hundred and eighty guests in for Christmas lunch. "I can do it, Craig," he says. "Give me the chance. Put me in charge." And being the soft cock I am, I gave in and allowed him the opportunity. I left that prick in charge for two minutes and people were getting Christmas pudding for their main course and Petit Fours with their fucking soup. I nearly shit my britches when Chef called me to come and save the sinking ship. Mike was nowhere to be found. One of the casuals walks up to me and says "I think there's a cat locked in the beer cellar. I can hear squealing." It was Mike."

"Bloody hell."

"I'm not an irrational person, but I will tear his face off and use it as a pizza topping if that fucker steps within twenty yards of me."

"That's not irrational at all."

"Why do they keep sending us hospitality graduates? They go to uni for three years, write essays and earn zero experience. Somebody asks for a coffee and they brown-squit in their pants."

By the time Craig's rant had come to an end, Mike was approaching from the far-end of the restaurant, looking more than a little stressed. Mike was short, fat and permanently red-faced, with eyes that were permanently set to "deer in the headlights". As he came towards us, and I prayed that he would keep walking.

"Erm… Craig…? The conference rooms need cordial… But I can't find the cordial… Can you help me find the cordial?"

I felt for Mike. If you were on Craig's shitlist, work was never going to be a pleasant environment for you. I had survived by having ambition and not pissing him off, but even being on his good side came with a side order of abuse. I could take it though. Mike couldn't.

Craig exploded.

"Get your fucking head together before I kick your cunt in!"

Craig's anger nearly blew Mike's wig off, and he ran out the back of the bar and towards the kitchen faster than Linford Christie with a jetpack. I took pity on him.

"Cordial is in the store cupboard next to Room 101, Mike."

A faint warble of a response came back from the kitchen.

"Thank you…"

"I think he's crying," I said, testing Craig's soul.

"He needs killing."

No hope for that soul.

Room 101 was every manager's favourite room. It was the room that was only used in an emergency, which meant that we had overbooked and a VIP didn't have a room, or a member of management had been caught cheating on their wives and needed a place to stay.

In the day, the Duty Manager used it to chill out, watch TV and make personal phone calls at no expense to them, which was what I was doing in there.

"So what's been happening?" I said, kicking my shoes off and making myself comfortable on the king-sized hotel bed, while making sure the phone didn't slide off the bedside table and fall on the floor.

"Nothing much. Buckley's lost some fur near his bum," Mum replied.

"Does it make him look more distinguished?"

"No. You shouldn't joke. What if he's ill?"

"Mum, he'll be fine. Buckers will live forever. How's Dad?"

"He's OK…"

That classic "I'm not going to tell you what's wrong but the tone of my voice will tell you that something is wrong" thing that all mums can pull off with aplomb. All you have to do to get the rest out of mum is be silent. The truth comes out eventually.

"He's been spending a lot of time at the office lately."

"Yep, he's having an affair," I said, in classic deadpan style.

Mum laughed so loud that I had to take the phone away from my ear, and I pulled the kind of face that constipated old men make whilst trying to let one go.

"Don't be ridiculous! Nobody else would have him. Saying that, I have noticed some strange activity on his credit card and a lot of scantily-clad girls have been swanning around the area."

"They're waiting for me to return, which I will soon, by the way. I do miss you guys, and Buckers. I'm constantly working at the minute. I never seem to have any time to do anything. All my time off is spent pissing about with Jim and Sean."

"Are they OK, bless 'em?"

"No. They're awful, awful, people."

"Aww, tell them I said 'Hello'."

"I will, Mum. I've actually got something to tell you."

"Ooh, sounds interesting…"

"I've been invited to a wedding."

"Oh wow! That's great news. You're getting older now. Your twenties and thirties are all weddings, weddings, weddings. Then it's all funerals after that. Bummer."

"Great, Mum. It's Lila Holmes' wedding."

I expected a gasp, a sharp intake of breath, or an Ennio Morricone score. What I got was…

"Who's that?"

What?

"Lila Holmes, Mum. Can't you remember her? Short, cute, cropped hair… She bought Buckley a ribbon-wrapped bone?"

"Oh, her!"

Only a dog owner would suddenly remember a person by being reminded of the gift they bought their mutt five years ago, when the beast could still see and didn't smell like feet.

"That's the one, Mum."

"She was wonderful! When you get the wedding list let me know and I'll chip in and we'll get one of the biggies!"

"Thanks for the enthusiasm, Mum."

"Are you not excited? Your generation are all growing up. Getting married, having kids."

"I guess I never looked at it that way, just how it affected me."

"Always so selfish. That's why you're in a bit of a spin. It's lovely to see people from your youth getting married though. More than a little surreal, too."

"Yeah, that must be it."

The phone started to break up and Mum started to get flustered on the other end.

"Oh, balls. Balls! Buckley's brought in a frog from the pond and let it go. It's jumping around everywhere. Can I call you back?"

"I'm calling from work, Mum."

"Later then?"

"Sure."

"Love you."

"Love you, too."

I could vaguely make out mum telling Buckley off as she trailed away and put the phone down.

I laid back on the bed and pondered what Mum had said about the whole 'generational' thing. She had a point. Would it have made any difference if it had been Jim or Sean that was getting married? Was it just the timing? The fact that Lila was going to be the first to get married?

After a fairly uneventful 11-hour shift, I arrived home around 7pm to the sight of Jim eating a yogurt in the hallway. You never get used to walking into your house and seeing a member of the British Army in full uniform, whether he's eating a Muller yogurt or not.

"Hey dude," he said.

"How's it going?"

"Good. I've got two days off."

"It seems weird that people in the army get days off."

"We all need time to recharge. Even terrorists must sit down and have a Cobra or two between plotting our fiery deaths."

"Nice."

"What are you up to?"

"Not much. I feel a bit weird today."

"Weird? Is it still the Lila thing?"

"Kind of. I spoke to my mum today…"

Jim perked up and butted in.

"Aww, how is Queen Chapman?"

"She's good mate, thanks… Anyway, she thinks that the whole funk I've gone into is because Lila is the first person to get married out of our generation."

"Yeah, could be. D'ya know what else it could be?"

"No."

Jim broke into song, putting the next line into the 'Five Gold Rings' section of '12 Days of Christmas'…

"Your complete, lack of baaaaaaaaaaaaaaaaaaaaaaaaalls!"

"Thanks for your support, as always."

I headed off to the living room, and plonked myself down in front of the TV. Before I could even switch it on, Jim had sat down next to me, and was looking at me with a smirk on his face.

"Look at how mopey you are. You need to add some spice to your life. Come and watch some porn with me. I've got some amazing stuff. It's like art, but, y'know, less gay."

"Art is gay, but watching porn together is 100% hetero?"

"100%."

"Fuck it, then. I do need cheering up."

"Excellent. Come on, buddy. I'll have you giggling like a girl in no time. I've got this film where there's a dozen burly bikers in a bowling alley, and this hot German girl just walks in naked and shouts "Hey guys, I want fuck!" It's hilarious."

"That does sound like art."

"C'mon you big ball bag."

Jim led me upstairs like he would one of his girls to watch a Pixar film. He was practically skipping. This was friendship to him, the crazy bastard. He took me into his room, which looked like a cross between a National Front disco and the bedroom of a fourteen-year-old boy: wall-to-wall England flags and Union Jack bed sheets, mixed in with film posters for *The Wild Geese* and *The Eagle Has Landed*. Oh, and a Bon Jovi poster for *Slippery When Wet*. The guy had serious taste issues.

Jim started a frantic search for the video, but to no avail. When he came out of his chest of drawers for air, he scratched his head and his face turned bright red. He looked like a man who had lost his wedding video, not one containing a circle-jerk session.

"Remind me to flick Sean's balls when I see him next," he said.

"Don't worry about it."

Jim stared at me for a moment, before sitting down and putting his arm round me.

"I think I'm starting to see what this girl meant to you, buddy," he said, his voice as calm as a whisper.

"I saw her a few weeks back, y'know," he continued, piquing my interest.

"Really? How did she look?"

"The same as before. She hasn't changed at all, really. Her hair has grown back a little. She didn't see me though. I had a perv and moved on."

"I wish she was fat."

"Fucking chubby chaser."

"No, dickhead. So I wouldn't care."

"Jesus, man. How much effort did you make to stay in touch with her? None. Look, it's weird for me, too. I disappear for six months at a time and I come back and everything is different. I could get called away to Iraq at any time and I know that if I do, things will be even weirder on my return. Sean could be in a relationship, for example…"

I laughed, and it made Jim smile. A little perspective is what you need sometimes.

"If you want my spin on this event, it's this: Lila wasn't for cock, she was for life. She was always going to fall in love and get married. I'm gutted you missed the boat, but there's a shit load more waiting for you."

"Thanks, man."

"Now relocate your balls and join me on a voyage of self-destruction tomorrow. Sean's off, and we're going to have a coffee in the morning at one of those wanky places you go to, before going and getting so drunk we don't know if it's New Year or New York. How's that for a chicken sandwich?"

"Sounds good. I'm supposed to be working tomorrow but I can switch with one of the other DM's and do one of their late shifts. They'll love me for it."

"Awesome. Now let's go and find that porn. We'll tear Sean's room apart. You check his panty drawers, I'll look under his vast collection of Attitude magazines."

After watching a horrendous film called 'Gangbang Debauchery', as Jim giggled along like you would to a Jim Carrey film, I needed some normality, which for me was playing *Fight Night*. I had loved boxing since I was a kid, and I played the game like I was a real boxer: dancing around, using my silky skills, everything coming off the jab.

Nothing annoyed Jim and Sean more.

They thought a boxing game worked in the same way as a *Street Fighter* game: hit the buttons as fast as you can until someone collapses in a heap. I toyed with them, left them flailing their arms like a drunk in the street, before knocking them out after five or six rounds of humiliation.

Suffice to say, they would rather play *Ecco the Dolphin* than challenge me with their primitive skills.

"I wish there was a cheat on this game where you could knock someone out with one punch. I would use it on you every fucking time," Jim said, looking over the top of his newspaper as I outboxed my on-screen opponent.

"You'd have to land the punch first, cock snogger."

Jim chuckled and burrowed his head back into his paper.

After a few moments, Sean's key turned in the lock and he entered the house, his mood instantly turning as soon as he saw me playing *Fight Night*.

"Oh for fucks sake, is he playing that again?"

"Hey Sean, I want fuck!" Jim shouted in his best impersonation of the German pornstar.

"Oh, you found 'Gangbang Debauchery'."

"Yeah, we found it underneath your Gary Glitter costume," I said.

"You're hilarious."

"Although it might have been a late-Elvis costume," said Jim.

"Very funny. If I had costumes, at least the arses wouldn't be cut out of them, you freak."

"He's got you there, man," I said.

I paused the game and put my hand up for Sean to high-five, which he did with pride.

"I don't know what you're laughing at," Jim said, turning to me. "You're in such as funk you have to beat up imaginary men to make yourself feel like a man."

"Whereas you just beat off to men," Sean chipped in.

"That was good, Sean. Fair play."

My attention went back to the game and quickly put an end to my opponent, using Lennox Lewis' big right-hand to put him down and out. Sean was not impressed.

"They should have Hasim Rahman on this game. He'd put Lewis to sleep again."

"Don't be silly. Rahman only beat Lewis because of the movie curse."

"What movie curse?"

Jim's newspaper came down, and he gave Sean a look that said, 'Now look what you've done'. Everybody knew that you didn't get me started on boxing. I'd talk your ears off.

"The boxers-in-movies curse. You didn't know there was one?"

"Enlighten me."

"Lennox Lewis was filming *Ocean's Eleven* when he should have been in Africa preparing for his fight with Rahman. Instead, he's hanging out with Clooney and co. whilst Rahman acclimatises to the African humidity. When it comes time to fight, Lewis is on his arse after two rounds, and in round five, he's *literally* on his arse."

Sean was intrigued, and wanted to know more.

"OK. Nice. But one boxer does not a movie curse make..."

"I'm glad you said that, sir. Wladimir Klitschko, who was filming *Ocean's Eleven* with Lennox, was sparked out by Corrie Sanders AND Lamon Brewster within a couple of years of being in the film."

"Hmm... you'll have to do better than that. He might've lost anyway."

"Fair enough. Antonio Tarver then..."

"Who?"

"AKA Mason Dixon in *Rocky Balboa*."

"I cried during *Rocky Balboa*," Jim said.

"What about him?" Sean asked, ignoring Jim's manly cry story.

"He was spanked by Bernard Hopkins in his next fight, and it was directly attributed to having to lose too much weight after the filming of Balboa. Movie. Curse. BOOM!"

Sean smiled, and nodded his head in appreciation of my knowledge in my chosen sport.

"You make a solid case, but in the grand scale of things, you still know more about sweaty men hitting each other than you do about life and women. I think that makes you what is known as a bit of a whopper."

Jim chuckled from behind his newspaper, before putting it down again.

"A-ha! Fuck your movie curse! How about Steve Collins appearing in *Lock Stock*?"

"A rare exception to the rule. He gets bonus points for spanking Chris Eubank twice."

Jim screwed his face up and gave me the finger.

"Enough of this. Sean, are you still up for going on an all-dayer tomorrow? Please say yes."

"Yes."

"Excellent."

"D'ya hear that, Jason? You're going to have a day off from bashing your bishop over Lila and men wearing gloves and shorts."

Sean laughed and slapped me on the back of the head, before heading off to change out of his work gear. I opted out of giving my opponent a rematch and opted to make dinner instead.

I used to cook all the time, but my shift patterns had made me lazy. I was always picking at food at work, too. When you work a 12 hour shift in a hotel, you could find yourself eating from breakfast, lunch and dinner buffets. If I stayed in this job past 30, I would be a right fat bastard.

I was looking forward to the drinking session. I needed to stop thinking about the past and concentrate on enjoying the present. Sean and Jim would certainly help me with the latter, even if it meant becoming lost in a shit-storm of booze.

Sean came back down from upstairs in his football gear, holding a huge netted bag filled with footballs. Perfect timing for Jim to tell a bad joke.

"Ah, Sean. I see you're still walking around the house holding your ball bag."

Right on schedule.

"Fantastic, Private Benjamin. I'm off to footy practice."

"Can I come?" I asked.

"Yeah, sure. May I ask why?"

"Just fancy getting some fresh air."

"There's no fresh air with sweaty teenagers around, buddy. But you're welcome to come along."

Truth be told, I liked to go along to Sean's practice sessions because they reminded me of when dad used to coach the local footy team back home. I was in the team two years below his, and it was nothing but good times. Watching Sean's lads run around swearing and taking the piss out of each other was like a time capsule, and a great distraction from everything else.

On the football field, Sean was a completely different beast to how he was at home. He ran around like a crazy person, barking orders at the young lads and knocking them into shape. I would be the worst disciplinarian ever. They'd take one look at me and think: "Bollocks!" before picking their noses, scratching their balls and talking about boobs and the Arctic Monkeys.

Sean didn't give them a second to think. It was actually quite endearing to see. He had a nickname for all of them and knew all their strengths and weaknesses.

"Oi, Sticky, try moving those gangly legs to and fro. It's called running."

"Two touches on the ball, Mickey Blue Eyes. That's a record, isn't it? Just messing with you. Good lad."

"You're not playing in the Italian league, Noodle. And you're not a seal, either. So stop rolling around, get up and get the ball back."

After 30 minutes of practicing skills and what the kids called "the boring stuff", Sean picked two sides and let the lads play against each other for the final 30 minutes. I used to love that bit as a kid. You could keep your stretches and your dribble-the-ball-around-some-posts game. I wanted to score some bloody goals! Nice to see that the next generation felt the same way.

Sean and I watched the game from the half-way line, and as Sean observed the lads and refereed the game, I took the opportunity to talk his ear off about Lila.

"What can you remember about me and Lila?" I asked.

"I remember that she drove you crazy."

"Crazy how?"

"You were too clingy. Too needy. You didn't know how to handle someone like her. But you were 16 and a big wet fanny. It's expected at that age."

Before I could respond to that comment, Sean was running up the pitch and blowing his whistle. A skinny ginger lad had just lunged in with a two-footed tackle, and the other lad had been sent flying through the air.

"Ginge, what are you doing? Diving in like a triple jumper. Run round the pitch twice and cool off, you animal."

Ginge headed off on his lap of dishonour, cursing Sean as he ran. Sean checked on the other lad and the game resumed when it became clear that he was a diving little shitbag just like the majority of senior players.

Sean walked back over to the halfway line.

"What were you saying, buddy?"

"Nothing mate. I'm just looking forward to tomorrow."

"Me too," he said.

7. Drink to Forget

Nothing sets you up for a day of permanent liver damage than a coffee served in a mug so big you could swim in it. Sean, Jim and I wandered into the local coffee shop and joined the queue. Jim had a look of utter disdain on his face, and muttered his disapproval under his breath, particularly at the penchant Sean and I had for going through the menu and cooing like a couple of old biddies. The long queue was clearly winding him up as well.

"When I was stationed in Hamburg, I noticed that Germans never queue," he said.

"Doesn't that create chaos?" Sean said.

"Out of chaos comes order," Jim replied.

Sean chuckled to himself.

"Two years stationed in Germany and he becomes a Nietzsche-quoting sociopath."

Jim frowned in confusion.

"Is that the guy from the start of Conan the Barbarian?"

Sean and I shared a "who just farted?" look, before turning our attention back to the menu.

"What's it to be, buddy?" I asked.

"Caramel latte with a sprinkle of cinnamon. Gotta be."

Jim looked more disturbed than ever, and this from a guy with more sex toys than an Anne Summer's party and a bedroom like a crime scene from *Seven*.

"You two make me sick. Black coffee. No sugar. No milk. You two are a couple of mocha-fuckers."

The queue shortened, and an attractive girl in her early twenties leaned over the glass counter filled with cakes and pastries holding a notepad.

"What can I get you, gents?" She asked.

Sean and I couldn't decide. Jim shook his head at us and ordered.

"Large black coffee, please."

The girl scribbled it down, before turning her attention to us. Jim couldn't help himself, putting on an old lady voice behind Sean's head.

"A cup of charisma and two balls, please."

The counter girl smirked, although she tried to hide it in the name of professionalism. Sean caught on to this and decided that being cool in this situation wasn't a realistic proposition.

"Two large caramel lattes, please."

We collected our brewskis and sat in the quiet section downstairs. All around us were people on their laptops.

"I bet a lot of terrible novels get written in coffee shops," he observed.

"So… What's the plan for tonight?" I asked.

"We destroy ourselves, and purchase a map so we can find your balls," Jim replied.

"You're obsessed with my balls."

"I feel like I've let them down by being out of the country for years at a time. I'm going to try and make it up to them for years of neglect."

"Awesome."

"He's kind of right," Sean chimed in. "We need to help you find your confidence again, and saying goodbye to Lila for good is the final part of the plan."

"The plan?" I smirked. "You two have a plan? I thought Jim just threw grenades at people and you chased kids around a field?"

"Ha-ha. Twat. Yeah, we have a plan. The plan is to get you out of the house and meeting people other than guests at the hotel. Hopefully some of those people you meet might want to play with your willy."

Jim snorted into his coffee at the use of the word 'willy', which further highlighted that I should be in charge of my own destiny.

"OK," I said. "What do you have in mind?"

"A series of dates. Jim's found a girl at the army centre who's dying to meet you."

"Jim's found a girl at the army centre? What are we going to do, dig trenches and do push-ups together?"

"That's awfully stereotypical of you," Jim said.

"What's she like?" I asked.

"Her name's Toni and she's a fitness fanatic. She's petite. She's cute. Completely nuts, like, but in a good way. Fiery."

"Yeah?"

I started to perk up.

"Uh-huh," Jim muttered, his arms now folded.

"Cool. Set it up."

"Oh, are you sure?" Jim said.

"Yes. And I apologise for the generalisation."

"That's OK."

"What else do you have in store for me?" I asked, turning to Sean.

"There's a girl at my work called Tina. She's quite cool. She's a bit of a tomboy, likes a beer and watches footy. Loves The Stone Roses..."

"Perfect!"

Jim pulled his bulldog face again.

"You want to date a Mancunian bloke?"

"Nah she's fit, man," said Sean.

"That's two dates, then," I said, optimistically.

"That's doubled your success rate for the last half a decade," Jim said.

"If only that wasn't kinda true..."

Jim necked his coffee like it was the last one he'd ever have.

"Let's get the fuck out of here before I enrol in art school, start wearing a scarf and download a Bloc Party album."

We headed for the exit, and as Jim walked past the tutting laptop owner, he peered over his shoulder and started narrating from the screen.

"No, Dad… I don't know how to love. You never taught me how."

The laptop guy smiled, but it was more out of fear and from having his personal space invaded than Jim's prank. If you're going to write in a public place and then expect the world to be quiet while you pen your masterpiece, you're asking for trouble. Especially with a muppet like Jim around.

Fortunately for our master plan – which comprised of little else than getting extremely drunk – the weather gods were smiling on us that day. When you're going to be drinking all day, it's nice to switch it up between indoor and outdoor drinking.

The Beech Tree was great because it had a nice backyard to booze in, and within ten minutes of their doors opening for service, we were making the most of it.

We sat down with three ice-cold pints of Grolsch, and Jim sparked up his first fag of the day.

"It makes no sense that you can be as fit as you have to be in the army and still puff on those things," Sean said.

"I don't smoke at all when I'm away. There's something about being on UK soil that makes me want to drink and smoke myself into an early grave."

"Yeah I get that," I said.

"In a good way, obviously…"

Jim gazed lovingly at his slowly burning cigarette.

"The Scots have started something. I can see a time when no one is allowed to smoke unless it's in your own home. That'll be a depressing day."

"I don't know, I think it'll be nice to come home from a night out not smelling like a tramp," I said.

Sean nodded in agreement. Jim looked at us both and shook his head.

"Mate, you have no idea. The amount of girls I've pulled just from smoking is crazy. Smoking breaks at work? Check. "Can I crash a fag, please?" as an ice-breaker? Check. Without smoking, I'd have to make more of an effort. And that's too much effort."

It was a good point. As much as I hated smoking, it was as social a habit as drinking. It made me think that Jim would have made a good politician. The scandal would be great to watch unfold. There would be no "I did not have sexual relations with that woman". It would be, "Who wants to see hidden camera footage of me having sexual relations with that woman?" and then he'd put his hand up, expecting to be high-fived by Andrew Marr or Nick Robinson.

"Let's change the subject," Jim said, shaking out of his smoke-filled depression. "Jason, what feels worse, the fact that Lila is getting married, or the fact that she's getting married at your work?"

"First of all, thanks for bringing it up. Secondly, I would say that having it at work is probably a good thing. It means that I won't get too drunk and make a twat out of myself."

"That's what you think," said Sean, causing Jim to splutter as he smoked.

"The whole venue thing isn't that big a deal. I've not told anyone at work about it other than Jane, and she's cool. She won't tell anyone. Other than that, I've just made a point of not being on shift whenever she has an appointment with the wedding co-ordinator, or if I am on shift, I make sure I'm hiding in a room somewhere watching a film."

"Don't you want to see her?" Sean asked.

"Not really. I'll just see her at the wedding."

"You're a strange boy," Jim said. "I'd want to break that ice before you turn up at the wedding of the one that got away. You might have a full-blown mental breakdown during the first dance. Which would be funny to watch, but we'd have to be responsible for you."

"Thanks for the concern. I'm sure I'll be fine."

Jim and Sean exchanged glances from across the rocking oak table. It was the look of concern, and I spotted it. I couldn't bring myself to try and convince them, especially now that I was spending most of my nights staring at the ceiling, whilst sifting through my memory for a reason as to why happiness in its purest form had passed me by.

Three or four pints passed, and the pub started to get busier. Five smartly-dressed women on their lunch breaks sat on a long picnic bench opposite us. Jim, who was facing them, made eye contact with one of the group. He kept smiling at her, and Sean and I bowed our heads, as we tended to do when the chance of conversation with the opposite sex occurred.

"Where do you guys work?" Jim called out to the woman.

She looked at her friends – possibly in the hope that they would shelter her from the weirdo talking to her – before smiling and calling back.

"Go Recruitment across the road."

"That's nice," Jim called back. "You all coming together."

"We all hate each other really," she replied, causing her workmates to boo and hiss at her.

"What are you guys doing? You've started early," she said, noticing our growing collection of beer glasses.

"My friend Jason here has just been invited to his ex-girlfriends wedding. It's smashed him to bits, so we're rebuilding him with beer."

"That's sweet of you."

Jim smiled, stood up and grabbed our empties.

"Three more?"

Sean and I nodded. Jim headed indoors to get us some more drinks. I felt the urge to turn round and acknowledge Jim's new friend, but I felt the fear creeping in. As for Sean, I don't think he could turn round. He was desperate not to break the seal and if he moved, he might release all over himself.

My cheeks were burning with anxiety. I knew that Jim had sown a seed for the woman to speak to us again, but I was terrified. If she was checking into the hotel or was complaining that her toilet wouldn't flush, I wouldn't have a problem. But once I was out of work and in a social environment, I couldn't disguise my complete lack of confidence.

Within a few minutes, Jim came back with three more drinks and sparked up another cigarette. "Aren't you going to thank me?" he said, popping another cigarette in his mouth.

"She's going to come over to this table before she goes back to work. She's going to say "Have a great time lads" or something, and she's going to turn to you and say "I hope it all goes well for you". When this happens, you have to say "Why don't I take you out sometime? It might take my mind off it.""

I stared across at Jim, my mouth partially open. I knew that there was no way that I was going to execute this half-arsed plan of his, even if she came over and said it word for word.

"I have to say, buddy, I'm impressed," Sean said, raising his glass to Jim before taking a gulp and grimacing in pain.

"Break the fucking seal, man!" I said.

"Oh thank God," Sean said. He stood up and waddled to the toilet like a constipated Ronnie Corbett.

Jim leaned towards me, his eyes wandering between me and the other table.

"She keeps looking over. It's definitely on."

"Great. What does she look like?"

"She's a brunette. Shoulder length. I'd say thirty-five years old. Keeps herself in shape. Dresses nice. Blue eyes, too. Brown hair and blue eyes is always attractive."

"I've got brown hair and blue eyes!"

"That's lovely, Jason. Let's not focus on our relationship right now."

I let out a belly laugh and took a sip from my pint. Knowing that the woman was 35 put me at ease. There was no way a mature woman was ever going to be interested in me, especially a career-minded one.

When Sean sat back down, it was with the relief of somebody who had shed half of their body weight.

"That was like the scene where Austin Powers gets defrosted," he said. "The guy next to me at the urinal thought I was asleep at one point. I was just staring at the ceiling with my eyes closed. It was close to a religious experience."

Jim shook his head and sat back in his chair to enjoy his cigarette, occasionally glancing over at the brunette from the opposite table and smiling at her. At this point, I wasn't sure if he was messing with me or freaking her out. Probably both.

Forty-five minutes later, I sensed the presence of somebody approaching from behind me, and my entire body tensed up. My eyes glanced over to my right, and the woman was there. She waved to Jim, then turned to me.

"Right. We're going back to work. You guys have a great time. I hope these two manage to put you back together," she said.

Wow, she was pretty.

"Thank you. I'm sure they will," I replied.

"Oh we'll take good care of him," Jim said, in a tone used only by serial killers.

"My name's Helen," the woman said, holding out her hand.

"Jason," I replied, accompanied by the limpest handshake known to man.

"I hope it all goes well for you."

Jim's eyes bulged out of his head, as if he was trying to will his thoughts into my brain. When I caught his gaze, I recalled what he had told me to say.

My mouth opened…

"Thanks."

Brain fart.

"Maybe I could take you out sometime? That'd be a much better way to get over it."

Better.

"Sure. Why not?" she asked.

"Because I'm a serial killer."

Silence.

Jim and Sean's heads dropped simultaneously.

Helen reached into her handbag, pulled out a business card, and handed it to me.

"Give me a call. If you survive," she said.

I took the card and put it in my shirt pocket.

"I will," I said.

Helen turned and walked away, and we watched as she joined her colleagues and disappeared from view. As soon as she did, I became eight years old.

"I'm going on a date with an older woman! Holy fucking shitballs!"

"Congratulations," Jim deadpanned.

I calmed myself down and took a victory swig from my pint. After a few moments, Sean chuckled to himself.

""Because I'm a serial killer…?""

I'm the kind of drinker who likes to find a great place with comfy seats and stay there all night. I've never really understood the point of 'bar crawls', unless you're with a large group. As most of my drinking sessions comprised of myself, Sean and Jim, we would usually end up in a maximum of three places over a night out, bookended with a coffee and a dodgy nightclub.

We had the perfect place for a settled-in session: The White House. A Wetherspoons-shunning mix of pop culture and eclectic furniture, you could find yourself sitting in a *Swingers* booth (the Jon Favreau movie, not the bring-your-wife-to-our-party kind) a comfy, padded section with a polished black table, or a barely-standing chipped oak table with one steel chair, one flea-bitten tub chair and a wobbly stool. It was part of its charm, and one of the reasons we used it so often.

"Plant yourselves. I'll get the drinks in."

Three or four hours passed, and our backsides were well and truly moulded into the cushioned booth of the pub. Jim's beer goggles were now firmly in place, and he returned from the bar with two girls and three pints. The two girls, in their early twenties and dressed casual in jeans and vest tops, sat down at the end of the booth with a bottle of wine and two glasses. Sean moved along so they could fit in.

"Gents, these two lovely ladies are Jo and Emma," Jim said. "They're studying… What was it again?"

"Creative Writing and Journalism," Jo said.

"Ah, that's cool," I said.

"What do you want to write about?" Sean asked.

"Assholes," Emma replied.

Sean nodded along, not sure how to respond to that one. Jim sat on the end of the booth next to the two girls and chucked at the word 'assholes' like it was the first time he'd ever heard it.

"Sounds interesting," I said.

I spotted that Emma was staring at Jim in an aggressive manner. I got the feeling that they had met before, and there was a good chance Jim was going to have his arse handed to him.

"Yeah," Emma continued. "I'm writing a 10,000 word story about a guy who spends entire evenings with girls, makes them feel really special by feeding them a story with zero foundation in truth, then sleeps with them and never calls."

The light switch turned on in Sean's brain, and we nudged each other under the table. We had ringside seats to Jim's comeuppance.

Jim, naturally, was oblivious...

"This story sounds hilarious!" he joked. "Maybe I could read a first draft later?"

Jo shoved Jim off the end of the booth so they could both get out, and Jim adopted his orphaned face.

"Hey, where are you going?"

"You! You are the asshole!" Emma said.

Jim, still confused, looked at me and Sean for clarification. We looked around the room, scratched our heads, picked up menus – anything not to acknowledge Jim.

"I don't understand?"

"You're the fucking asshole!" Emma hit him with that word again.

"Wait..." Jim said.

The hamster that processes information in Jim's head started to run in its wheel.

"Do I die in the end?"

"I fucking hope so!" Emma said, storming over to another section in the bar where she wouldn't see us anymore. Jo followed, shaking her head in disgust.

Jim watched the girls walk away with a dumbstruck expression on his face. Sean and I started laughing, which brought Jim out of his fog and back to reality. He sat back in the booth and scratched his head, searching for answers.

"I can't believe that instead of saying 'sorry', you asked how the story ended. You absolute bellend," Sean said.

"I can't remember her at all," Jim said. "We've got to stop coming here. I can't keep having uni students using me for their own academic gains."

Talk about missing the point.

It was only right that we spared Jim from meeting anyone else who had written a dissertation about how much of a twat he was to them. We moved on to another part of town, and over the next few hours, consumed a ridiculous amount of booze over four different venues.

1am was time for Feedback, a nightclub for fans of sticky dancefloors, cheap drinks and indie music. Perfect for three bleary-eyed twenty-somethings who at this point could barely walk and talk. Who needs to when you're dancing to Suede and the Happy Mondays in a room full of likeminded people?

We joined the queue outside the nightclub, and composed ourselves so we would stand more of a chance of getting in. It was going to be a struggle to get past the two doormen unless we stayed together, but Sean had already wandered off. Jim and I leaned on each other in a bid to remain upright and walking straight. That seemed to work.

Until we got to the door.

The two doormen stood in front of us.

"Sorry, lads, not tonight," the biggest one said.

Jim stepped forward.

"C'maaaaaan! Let us shin," he slurred.

"No," the doorman responded. "And it ain't 'cause you're both pissed."

Jim smirked and cockily shrugged his shoulders.

"Oh, I geddit. It's wall-to-wall chorizo in there. Not enough girlies?"

"No. It's 70% girls in there. That's our quota."

Jim started to get agitated, despite the fact that if you breathed on him hard enough, he would fall like a tree.

I stared at my shoes and wished that I could click my fingers and be transported to my bed.

"Is it because you think we might be trouble?"

Jim puffed his chest out – at least as much as he could without passing out or throwing up all over himself. This brought a smile to the biggest doorman's face. He chuckled before gently turning Jim to his right.

"It's because your friend is pissing up the wall of the club," he said, pointing to a wobbly Sean peeing up a wall like a five-year-old child using a urinal by himself for the first time. "And I'm offended by his tiny penis."

"You and me both, sir," Jim quipped.

It was time to admit defeat. We stumbled out of the queue, took hold of Sean's arms and led him home through the streets of Leicester.

8. The Breakfast Club

William Blake once said: "Think in the morning. Act in the noon. Eat in the evening. Sleep in the night."

Great rules to live by, unless you've drank your bodyweight in Grolsch in the evening and are then woken up at stupid o'clock by a man in a pair of red boxer shorts.

"Wake up, Latte Boy!" Jim shouted, jumping up and down on my bed.

"Fush off," I replied, my face still planted in my pillow.

"You're too young to have hangovers. Let your spirit free, it's the only way to be."

I gazed over to my alarm clock. It was 6:27am.

"I'm not in until midday. Leave me alone. Sleepies…"

Jim stopped jumping on the bed and leapt onto my bedroom floor. I could feel him watching me still, so I made sure I had one eye on him. He looked serious.

"If you fall asleep, I'm going to teabag you."

I decided that it was in my best interest to get out of bed. I rose up, shook the cobwebs off and adjusted my eyes to the waking world.

"Sean's making bacon sandwiches," Jim said.

I listened out for the incredible sound of sizzling pig… Yup, there it was, and the smell followed quickly. As I passed Jim, he kicked me up the backside.

"Nearly lost a toe," he joked.

"Shut up you weirdo," I replied, grabbing a pair of shorts and a T-shirt from the back of the chair as I left the room.

Jim and entered dining room, which was more of a dump with a table and four chairs in it than an actual dining room. Everything that wouldn't fit in the living room, including book shelves, CD, DVD and VHS storage, and unopened boxes filled with kitchen appliances that our parents had bought us as housewarming gifts but were never used.

We sat down at the dining table and cleared it of all the clutter we had accumulated over the last few months. Sean walked out of the kitchen holding three plates, each one containing a huge bacon sandwich.

"I thought you'd be wearing your pinny?" Jim said.

"I thought you'd be wearing your butt-plug," Sean fired back.

Jim laughed, before drowning his bacon sarnie in ketchup.

"Are you morons going to tell me why we're up at this ridiculous hour?" I asked.

Sean and Jim looked at each other and smirked, which made me nervous.

"What?" I asked.

"Well…"

Anything that starts with a 'well' is not going to be good news, particularly when it came from Jim's mouth.

"Luigi called this morning. The DM has had to go home sick. They need you to come in and cover the breakfast rush. I told him you would. Hence why I woke you up."

My heart sank.

"Are you crazy? I can't fucking see. I smell like a brewery and just looking at this bacon sandwich is making me want to spew all over the table."

"You'll be fine, you big fanny," Jim replied, with zero sympathy.

"I'll drive you to work, don't worry," said Sean.

"Oh that makes me feel so much better," I said, noting that Sean looked almost as terrible as I did.

"I feel quite good. I've had a coffee and a poo and I'm ready to rock," said Sean.

The word 'poo' alone made the contents of my stomach attempt to make a bid for freedom.

"Get your shit together and we'll go."

Eight minutes and forty-seven seconds later, I was sitting in the car with Sean. The car was rocking like we were in the Amazon rainforest, not driving down a straight road in Leicester. It didn't help that Sean had the radio on full blast, and he was singing along to 'I Wanna Be Sedated' by The Ramones – badly – and putting in his own words whenever he struggled to recall the real ones.

"Twenty-Twenty-Twenty-four hours to gooooooooooo, I wanna be sedated. Nothing to do, nowhere to go-oh-oh, I wanna be sedated. Put me on an airport, put me on a plane. Hurry, hurry, hurry, I love you Billy Zane. I feel it in my fingers, I feel it in the drain. Oh-oh-oh-oh-ohhhhhhhhhhhhhhhhhh…"

If the police had stopped us, the breathalyser would have fucking exploded.

The car screeched to a halt outside the hotel, and I managed to haul myself out of Sean's car. I slammed the door – mainly in protest of Sean's singing – and tottered towards the doors of the hotel. Acid reflux had set in, and I was burping every few seconds. I also had beer sweats, which is never good when you're wearing a white shirt underneath your suit jacket and your short hair means that your shiny, sweaty forehead stands out a mile away.

I made my way through the hotel lobby and towards the restaurant, which by this point was full of families, business folks and people as drunk as me. At full capacity, the restaurant held 150 people, and the hotel was full every day bar Sunday at this time of year, which meant that service had to be quick and efficient. The Duty Manager's job during breakfast was to flit between helping the reception out with check-outs, and ensuring that the restaurant staff weren't getting behind. Most of the time, this comprised of taking trays filled with plates – which were covered in half-eaten food – into the kitchen, scraping the food into the waste chute and then loading the Kitchen Porter's conveyor belt with dirty plates.

I was not looking forward to this, as one bacon sandwich nearly provided my undoing. An entire tray could finish me off.

I stumbled past Cathy, the restaurant supervisor, and she looked at me out of the top of her glasses and sighed.

"You smell like a bar cloth. Are you OK?"

"No," I replied. "Where do you want me?"

"The girls are struggling with the trays. They're filling up. Can you take them through?"

"Sure," I said.

The huge trays were full to the brim with plates. They were only supposed to take half this amount, but the girls were getting their arses kicked enough as it was. They didn't need Oliver Reed turning up and sweating all over them as I told them off.

I grabbed the first tray and lifted it off the counter. Not too heavy, I thought. But the strain of carrying it made me belch, which sadly travelled down into the face of a young boy who was eating with his parents. He pulled a face that is usually reserved for people picking up dog shit for the first time, and turned to his dad.

"Eww, Dad. That man just burped on me," he said.

"Be quiet and eat your expensive pancakes," the dad responded, saving me from having to stop walking and apologise for my abusive wind.

I burst into the kitchen holding the tray and made it to the Kitchen Porter's section by the skin of my teeth. From behind me, I could feel Sai and his cronies watching me from the pass, their beady eyes staring at me from under the heat lamps.

Sai called out to me when he realised I was sweating like Wayne Rooney reading a Saga brochure.

"Hey there, Sweaty Betty!" He shouted.

I ignored him, choosing to focus on my job in the hope that concentration would steady the ship.

"Get a whiff of all of that half-chewed meat, the stale bread and pancakes, the maple syrup soaked waffles, the…"

I took the bait.

"Fuck off!" I shouted.

The chefs broke into hysterical laughter.

"Black pudding and piss-flaps all round," Sai continued.

I couldn't hold it in any longer. My stomach attempted its own version of Johan Cruyff's famous turn from the 1974 World Cup, and I projectile vomited into the waste chute like a champion.

The chef's roared with delight at my misfortune, and I felt a little better after emptying my guts.

Suddenly the kitchen went deadly silent.

I twisted round, only to be faced with the General Manager of the hotel, holding a small empty plate. A bead of sweat crawled down my nose and fell onto my shoe, and before I could say anything, a line of dribble from my bottom lip followed suit.

What could I do in this situation? I couldn't laugh and joke with him about this, and I certainly couldn't fake an illness because I smelled like Billy Idol's dressing room. I did what anyone would do in that situation: I took the plate from his hand and placed it on the conveyor belt.

"Morning," he said, looking at me like I'd walked into his house naked and slapped his wife around the face with my balls.

And that was it. He walked back to his office to write himself a reminder to ask Craig to give me the bollocking of my young working life tomorrow.

I gave Sai and his crew a defiant shrug of my aching shoulders.

"Could've told me he was there," I said.

I took my jacket off to continue scraping the food from the collection of plates. The sweat had now completely consumed my white shirt, and Sai came over to inspect me.

"Jesus Christ, man. Why are you sweating so much? Are you on amphetamines?"

"What? No! Of course not. You think I'd come to work looking and smelling like this if I was on speed? I'd be hugging everyone and licking the roof of my mouth."

"Either way, you might want to practice sucking cock. You're going to need it."

I nodded in agreement, and Sai headed back to his band of grinning hyenas.

"And put your jacket back on. You look like Simon Le Bon in 'The Reflex' video."

Usually I'd have taken that as a compliment, but Sai was right. The shirt was best kept under wraps. I finished off scraping the plates and headed back to the kitchen for round two. Best to keep going and deal with the fall out of my puke-fest later, I thought.

I grabbed the next available tray of plates from the restaurant, eager to make amends and keep busy, but the heavier side of the tray slid a little, and in my panic, I stepped forward onto a half-eaten sausage, which caused me to slip back and fall on my arse. I watched in super slo-mo as the entire tray of plates and wasted food came crashing to the ground, with the vast majority of the food – baked beans, mushrooms, ketchup, brown sauce, bacon fat and eggs of the scrambled and fried variety – landing on my groin, stomach and chest area. Every single plate broke in the fall, and my heart stopped beating.

I rose to my feet, the food sliding and dropping off my clothes and onto the floor, like the guys attempting to hold on to the Titanic as it plunged vertically into the ocean. Right there, in that moment, I'd rather have been one of those unfortunate bastards.

The entire audience of 150 people stopped eating, talking and even breathing to stare at me as I got back to my feet. Staff included. Nobody knew what to say or do, and as I stood there, covered in Ikea fragments and tinned tomatoes, all I felt was pain. The pain of realisation that while Lila was visiting florists, cake-makers and booking her honeymoon, I was carrying plates to a kitchen whilst hungover to buggery.

I looked down at the broken plates, which now resembled my life in a weird, fourteen-year-old-attempting-to-write-poetry-for-the-first-time kind of way, and then up to see a young man standing in front of me, his face a mixture of sympathy and anticipation that I might have a mental breakdown and murder his family with a Cumberland sausage and half a side plate.

"Are you OK?"

There's no coming back from this, I thought. After a few seconds of composure, I opened my mouth to speak.

"Eat your breakfast..."

A pause that seemed to last a lifetime.

"...And go fuck yourselves."

Craig entered the small conference room holding a bottle of still mineral water and a glass filled with ice. He put them down in front of me and pulled his chair closer to the table. I started to chuckle to myself.

"What's so funny?" Craig asked.

"He sends you to sack me instead of doing it himself. It's a joke."

"Shit rolls downhill, you know that. I should've got Mike Twathouse to do it... Who would've carried that tray better than you did, I might add."

I smiled, before filling my glass with water.

"Did you already have those clothes here?" he asked, looking at my crumpled jeans and hoodie combo.

"Yeah. They've been here for months actually, stuffed in my locker in case I ever went out straight after work. I guess I won't be needing that locker anymore."

"Of course not, you're fucking fired."

"Thought as much."

"Yeah, 'gross misconduct'. Mike is taking your place, you dick. Now I'm guaranteed a public meltdown, too. Or a public execution for that cunt."

I bowed my head and enjoyed my ice cold water for a moment as I let my first ever sacking sink in. Craig looked at me closely.

"Don't beat yourself up too much. You've got a decent exit story out of it, and I'm sure it won't hold you back. You're a bright lad. You're just not cut out for this industry. Go and find something you actually wanna do and put your heart and soul into it."

Craig's speech was surprisingly profound, considering his track record for expletives, death threats and horrendous put-downs.

"I wish I'd seen you fall. I'd have pissed my pants."

Normal service was resumed.

"What was it like, having to be escorted out of the restaurant by Sai?"

"I don't know which was more surreal, the fact that 150 people started throwing food at me when I was already covered in it, or the looks I got from the guys in the locker room who hadn't started their shifts yet, who watched me take off a suit made from breakfast."

Craig started chuckling, and that slowly grew into a full belly laugh.

"Fucking hell. Let's get you out of here."

"Are you going to kiss me at the door?"

"Only if you let me send the CCTV footage to 'You've Been Framed'."

"Give me half of the £250 and you've got yourself a deal."

"I'd rather keep the video to remind myself of what a twat you are."

We left the conference room and took the lift down to the lobby. As the lift doors opened, Jane was walking back to the bar holding a round black tray which she'd used to deliver some cappuccinos to some wanker bankers in the lobby. She walked over and gave me a kiss on the cheek, followed by a gentle mumsy squeeze.

"Are you OK, darling?" she asked.

"I'm fine."

"That's good to hear. They're just about finished clearing up after you. I think you're going to be talked about for a long time."

"I always knew I'd become famous one day."

"For being a dippy bastard," Craig muttered under his breath.

"Use this as a springboard to something better, OK?" said Jane.

"I will," I said. "Spit in the GM's cappuccino for me, OK?"

Jane slapped me on the arm with her tray and walked back to the bar. I was going to miss my chat-and-espresso mornings with her. Plus I'd have to pay for my coffees from now on.

I took a second to gaze around the hotel lobby and reception area.

"I've been thinking about leaving this place for about three years," I said.

"I've been wishing you'd leave this place for about three years," Craig responded.

"Thanks man," I said.

"Look man, you'll be alright. Go and travel. Meet some people. Go crazy. There's no excuse for being a mopey fucker in your twenties. Wait until you're like me, a miserable fucker who hates everyone."

"Will do," I said. "I hope I didn't let you down."

"Only because you didn't decapitate any customers with that tray you dropped. Now fuck off before I make you hand wash your suit."

"Fuck you."

"That's Mike's job now."

Craig punched me on the arm and walked back towards the restaurant and kitchen, no doubt to have a piss-take at my expense and to hand out some free coffee vouchers to people who were still moaning about my little outburst.

I exited the hotel and felt the sunshine of a day that had only just begun. The sacking hadn't yet sunk in, and I knew that when it did, I would have an anxiety attack of gargantuan proportions. But until then, I thought, I'm going to enjoy the sunshine, have a nice slow walk home, and concentrate on getting back into the world.

I reached into my wallet and pulled out Helen's business card. I figured that a date with an attractive older woman was a good a place to start on my road to recovery. All I needed now was the balls to call her.

I took the longest walk home, even stopping to watch some ducks and swans in the nearby park. It was like I'd been released from prison, not sacked from a hotel. The weight of the world had been lifted from my shoulders. If I was going to turn up at the wedding unemployed – not to mention the fact that I might not be able to get into the venue due to having just being sacked from there – I would have to commit to finding a plus one. Starting right now.

When I arrived home, Jim was laying on the sofa, still wearing nothing but his red boxer shorts.

"You're home early," he said. "Did you soil yourself?"

"Kind of." I replied.

Jim sat up and turned round.

"But you left here in a suit. I vividly remember laughing at how sweaty you looked in it."

"I don't need the suit anymore," I said, a triumphant smile forming.

"What happened?"

"I dropped an entire tray of plates and food on myself. Then I told an entire restaurant of customers to go fuck themselves. Then I was politely escorted from the premises."

Jim jumped up onto the sofa and started jumping and cheering. He looked like a homeless, crack-addled ex-dancer who was attempting a comeback with his own interpretation of *Flashdance*.

"Holy fucking shitballs, that's fanny-tastic!"

"It's not *that* fantastic."

"Oh but it is, dear boy," he said. "It is 100% pure genius. I'm so happy for you. That job was part of the reason you're in this funk. Let's celebrate."

"I think I'm going to go to my parents for a few days. I've neglected them for a while."

"Ah, I get it. Creature comforts and cuddles from your ma. Makes sense, buddy. Makes sense. You go and enjoy yourself, and pinch your mum's bum for me."

"OK, buddy."

Jim's excitement made me laugh, and as I headed for the kitchen, I could see that Sean was bringing in his clothes from the backyard.

"Proud of you," Jim called out from the other room.

Bless him.

In the garden, a glum looking Sean was unpegging his designer briefs from the clothes line, before folding them and balancing them on his shoulder.

"Hi, mate," I said.

"What are you looking so cheery about?"

"Ah, nothing much. Y'know."

"What?"

"Got sacked today."

"Oh fuck," he said. "I'm sorry."

"Why?" I asked.

"I answered the phone this morning and said you'd come in. It's my fault."

"It's the best thing you ever could have done for me."

"Really?"

"Really."

"You're weird."

"I know."

Sean threw his collection of briefs onto a larger pile inside the kitchen door and came back to start collecting his socks.

"What are you so down about?" I asked.

"Jim's been stealing my socks and wanking into them. They're like fucking cardboard."

"Nice."

"Honestly, you could take them to Lords and hit sixes with them."

He threw one to me. I could have thrown it at the wall and took out a brick with it.

"What are you going to do with them?" I asked, knowing that Sean was likely to spend £50 on five pairs, whereas I would buy 50 pairs for £5.

"Choke him to death with them," he said, only half joking. "Or I might use it for the bar scene of my low-budget remake of *Out for Justice*."

"You wouldn't need to put snooker balls in these bad boys," I said, throwing it back to him. "I'm going to head to my parents for a few days. I'll catch up with you soon."

"Nice one, buddy. Give that Helen a call, too. She seemed nice. Wedding's coming up, soon."

9. From Despair to Where?

I passed my driving test when I was seventeen years old: Four minors, emergency stop, three-point turn and reverse parking. No worries. Easy peasy. Mum and dad patted me on the back, took me out for dinner and I dutifully sent off for my licence.

That was the last time I had anything to do with a car.

I was never interested in driving; I was simply fed up with dad whingeing at me about "freedom" like a low-rent Mel Gibson. I figured that if I passed, I could go back to not being moaned at. I've always loved public transport, and as I sat on the train back to the old town, I stared out of the window at the rows of terraced houses and open fields, thinking about the wedding and what the hell I was going to say to my parents about the job.

I knew that they wouldn't care about the sacking, it was what I planned to do next that they would worry about. They wouldn't want me to be completely directionless – or unemployed, for that matter – they'd want me to find something that paid the bills and made me happy. Problem was, I didn't have the foggiest what that would be. I opted for the lying-through-my-teeth approach for now.

The train pulled into the station, and as I jumped up and grabbed my rucksack, I noticed a vaguely familiar face grinning at me from down the carriage. It was Amy, a girl who was on the Leisure and Tourism course with me, and had passed with flying colours and – shock horror – actually got a job in Leisure and Tourism as a Travel Agent. She was a close confidante at college, and always game for a laugh.

"Jason Chapman, as I live and breathe!" she said theatrically, running down the carriage and throwing her arms around me.

I kissed the top of her head, which was buried into my chest, and jumped off the train and onto the platform with her still attached to me. Why didn't every attractive girl greet me like this?

"How are ya? I've not seen you for donkeys'," she said.

"I'm good, thanks. How've you been?"

"Ah, y'know... Still working in travel. What are you up to these days?"

"I've been working at the Hunters hotel in Leicester. Long hours, which is why I haven't been here for so long. Feels weird."

"I bet. Are you going to Lila Holmes' wedding?"

"Yeah," I said, surprised that anyone outside of my own head was attending the wedding.

"Thank God," said Amy, putting her hand to her mouth. "As soon as I opened my mouth, I thought, "Fuck!" in case you hadn't been invited."

"Ha! Nope, you're fine," I said.

"That was lucky!"

"Are you going?" I asked.

"Yep. I've known her twenty years. Two schools and one college. I haven't seen her in a long time though. I'm very much in the 'box ticked' camp."

"Me too," I said, desperately hoping that it wasn't the case. "If I remember rightly, you never approved us being together?"

"You're right. We were so close, and I didn't like that you dropped your friends at a second's notice if she clicked her fingers. Naturally, you've mentally blocked out all of the crap things she did?"

"Yeah... she was an angel."

We shared a laugh, and for a moment it was like we were still at college. I'd wasted so much time working my arse off for no reason.

Amy's phone bleeped and she tapped at the buttons as fast as she could.

"How rude of me. Sorry about that," she said.

"Not at all. Boyfriend?"

"Fiancée."

"Wow. I really am going to be the last one on the shelf."

"Don't be silly. So what brings you back to these parts?"

"I've come to raid my Mum and Dad's cupboards."

"Bless 'em. I love your folks. How is your Mum now? I heard she'd been ill?"

"The nervous breakdown thing?"

Amy gave me a classic schoolteacher-telling-off-a-pupil-with-her-eyes-from-across-the-classroom look. I'm sure it has a shorter name. Either way, it worked.

"Sorry. I get a little defensive."

"There's no need. Is she feeling better?" she asked.

"She will do. I'll give her some TLC."

"You're sweet," said Amy, giving me another hug.

"I try," I said. "I've got no job and nothing better to do."

"Don't play the big man. You're here because you want to be. You're a good person. I won't ask about the job though."

"For another time, that one."

"Good idea. Let's meet up again while you're down here? Unless you're super busy."

"Sure. Give me your number."

I took my phone out of my pocket. Before I could do anything, Amy snatched it from me and stored her number in it.

"I expect a call very soon," she said.

"And you'll get one. Say hi to Dave for me. It is Dave you're marrying, right?"

"Yes!"

"Wow. I could've opened up some old wounds there," I said, the panic waning.

"Like how you lost your job?"

"Leave."

Amy laughed as I pointed to the exit and put on my best 'faux insulted' face expression. A career in acting would not be forthcoming.

"I'll see you soon, you sexy beast," she said, punching me in the stomach before walking off down the platform.

"Definitely," I said.

The walk to my parents' house was a mixture of nostalgia and surrealism. When you're a kid, everything seems huge. Streets that seemed to go on for miles are now walked in a matter of seconds, and all the houses, parks and shops seem to shrink with age. It had only been six months since I'd been home, but it felt like twenty years.

The last time I was there, mum told me off for knocking instead of just walking in. "You lived here for 18 years. This will always be your home," she said. I comprised on this occasion by entering the house and then knocking.

"Hellooooooo," I said. "Mum? Dad? Buckley?"

I crept in and kicked my Airwalks off at the door. The fourth, eighth and twelfth stairs had creaked since 1994, and dad had sworn to put them right ever since. When I heard one of them creak, I popped my head around and saw mum cautiously walking down the stairs.

"What are you looking so nervous about? It's only me," I said.

"I know it is!" Mum said, snapping out of her nerves and hurrying towards me.

She threw her arms around me like she hadn't seen me in years.

"Bloody hell, Mum. You can't have missed me that much?" I said.

"I always miss you," she replied. "And the days seem longer when you miss someone."

Mum was a long-distance runner in her youth, and she still looked pretty athletic. She'd been through a tough time of late, and it had aged her, but she still looked better than most people her age. She went into the kitchen to make some tea, and I sat down in the living room and looked for signs that dad had done any of the decorating he'd talked about doing for half my lifetime. A lick of magnolia, a few new photo frames and a large print of Turner's *The Morning after the Wreck*. Apart from that, same as it ever was.

Mum entered the living room holding a full tea tray: cups, saucers, milk jug, teapot and a plate of biscuits.

"I feel one hundred years old," I joked.

"You look it," Mum said, putting the tea down on the pine coffee table.

"I've never seen such huge bags under such a young person's eyes."

"That's because I'm living the dream, Mum. I'm out every night. Different girl each time. Alcohol instead of water…"

"More like you're working too many hours at that hotel," she said.

"Yeah, that's the truth."

"How do you feel about the wedding now?" Mum asked.

"I'm OK. I think you were right. It's given me a kick up the arse… sorry, bum, to do something special. I think I'm going to go travelling after the wedding."

The words came out of my mouth as if the result of an enema. Mum smiled, albeit with a hint of sadness, and poured us both tea.

"You'll be gone for even longer then," she said, passing me my cup.

I grabbed a biscuit and went for the dunk. Anything to give my brain enough time to process the spontaneous life plan that had burst out like Tourette's.

"I won't be gone forever," I said.

"Where do you think you'll go?" Mum asked.

I wracked my brain for a quick and easy answer. For reasons that could only be attributed to the fact that I'd been recently been living in 1997, I thought of the Manic Street Preachers.

"Australia," I said. "I'm going to spend a year in Australia."

"Have you looked into flights, visas, and all of that stuff yet?" Mum asked.

"All under control, Mum. All under control."

The only info on Australia I had were a list of things that kill you: crocs, spiders, snakes, Michael Hutchence. Other than that, I knew nothing bar the fact that it sounded like a good idea, considering I'd only hatched it seconds ago.

"So where are Dad and Buckley?" I said, changing the subject.

"Rutland Water. He'll be back any minute."

I detected a mood change when I mentioned dad. He wasn't around when I had called the other day, and he wasn't here now. Something wasn't right.

The front door opened suddenly. I jumped out of my skin, and mum almost ended up gripping the chandelier like a Tom and Jerry cartoon. She closed her eyes and put her hand on her heart.

Dad walked into the living room holding two pairs of shoes, one of which were mine. He looked at me from across the room and frowned, and I noticed that he'd grown at least two chins since the last time I saw him, although you could barely see them under his late-Eighties Gerry Adams beard.

"Your shoes, I presume?" he said.

"Hello, Dad. Nice to see you, too."

"Hmm."

All dads hum, groan or sigh their displeasure at things. He walked through the kitchen and into the adjacent garage, and I heard my shoes being thrown into a heap. Mum looked at me and rolled her eyes. He doesn't change much.

Buckley – named after the late, great Jeff – came sprinting into the room and into my arms. He was a golden retriever, with the longest, curliest hair. He would've been the model for many bands of the Seventies. Robert Plant would've killed for those locks.

Mum watched me wrestling Buckley as I talked to him in a code that only pet owners wouldn't find weird. She jumped up and got an extra cup and saucer for Dad, who came in and plonked himself down his special chair next to the TV. Neither of them acknowledged each other, which was out of turn. Dad had always given mum a kiss or a squeeze around the hip before.

"What have you been up to, Jay? Keeping busy?" he asked, breaking me out of my daydream whilst flicking through the Sky Sports channels.

"Not much. Dealing drugs. Pimping. Ultra-violence. Cabbages. Knickers. It doesn't have a beak."

Dad turned to me.

"I am listening to you," he said, before turning back to the TV.

"Just checking," I said. "I'm not up to much. I was just telling Mum actually… I'm thinking of going travelling for a year. To Australia."

It still sounded ridiculous.

"Australia?"

Dad's voice went a little higher when he said that, but it didn't cause him to throw the remote at me or shake his head in dismay at what a directionless moron I was, which was kinda what I expected.

"Make sure you've got plenty of cash saved and you sort your visa out properly," he said. "And I wouldn't bother fruit picking whilst you're out there. A mate from work's daughter went out there and was bitten by a redback. She ignored it and within an hour she was sweating and hallucinating. Then she collapsed…"

Typical dads. Anything you suggested, someone had either died or failed miserably at it.

"Well now I'm definitely going…" I joked.

"Just saying. It's a lot of hours in the sun for terrible money."

"Sounds like my situation now. Minus the sun, sadly."

"Good luck with it, son."

Mum placed the cup and saucer down on the small table next to dad's chair. He didn't say a word. I hate rudeness, so I had to bite my lip again. Dad's abrupt, and he'd never win any comedy awards, but he wasn't rude. Something was up.

Mum sat down and Buckley left me and lay under her legs. He peeped out at me through her shins like they were prison bars.

I sprawled on the sofa with my tea and biscuits. This was what coming home was all about: creature comforts.

I'd be climbing the walls within minutes.

Four hours of being with your parents when they hardly talking to each other is enough to drive anyone mad. I sent Amy a text message about meeting up, and she asked me if I'd like to go and see Ed, our old college tutor.

I felt a rush when I read the text. Nostalgia fest! Lila's wedding – with all the emotions and memories that brought up – then coming home for the first time in ages and seeing Amy, and now going back to the old college again. The scene of so many good and bad times. It had to be done.

My sleeping habits returned to their post-invitation shiteness that night, only this time it was because I was excited about seeing Amy and going to college, rather than drowning in a sea of regret and negativity. Ed was a great tutor, albeit one that taught us nothing. He was a great tutor in that he loved The Smiths, Stone Roses and had seen The Happy Mondays at The Hacienda back in 1987, where he said that he took so much speed that he spent the whole night terrified that his penis was going to go up inside his body and never return. Naturally, we thought this was hilarious.

Ed would talk about music and film for hours, then realise that he'd taught us fuck all that lesson and apologise to the people who had turned up to learn something, before giving us a bollocking for distracting him. How he was still teaching was anyone's guess. Amy said he was a course leader now. In what, Madchester Studies?

Amy was waiting for me at the college gates, like Lila used to back in the day. We gave each other a big hug and walked up the winding driveway up to the mobile classrooms that Ed now called home. We were giddy with excitement at seeing Ed again.

"I meant to ask you last night, how did you get in touch with Ed?"

"MySpace. Are you on it?"

"Fuck no. Looks weird."

"It is weird, but a few friends got me on it and I've got back in touch with some of the old guys because of it. Then Ed added me and we've chatted a few times since. This is the first time I'd have seen him since we left though."

Ed hadn't changed a bit. He will forever be the raver who suddenly found himself having to wear a suit to go to work. The tiny acts of defiance were there though; his tie was loose, the hair ruffled and unkempt, the top button undone on his shirt. It wouldn't have surprised me if there was a 'Made of Stone' T-shirt on underneath.

"Mr Chapman, how the devil are you?"

Ed was losing his Nottingham accent fast. He'd be a full-on country bumpkin before long.

"Good man, how are you? And more importantly, how the fuck are you, Course Leader?"

"Still a cheeky bastard," he said, turning to Amy. "Hello my lovely."

"Hi, Ed!" Amy said.

"Come in and sit down in the classroom. 100% pure nostalgia."

Ed was enjoying his little showaround. He took us inside the mobile classroom – which sounded so hollow that if you jumped hard enough, I'm pretty sure the entire place would fold like the house at the end of *Poltergeist* – and made us a coffee using a range of supplies that looked like they belonged in a crack den rather than a classroom.

Amy and I sat in our old classroom and the memories came flooding back. The guys used to lock each other in the store cupboard. I took a girl named Emma in there for a snog and a fumble once, too. Wow, we had some good times in here, I thought. Amy went over to the blackboard, grabbed the tiniest piece of chalk available and wrote the words 'JASON IS A BALL BAG' in big letters.

"You always used to do that," Ed said, walking back in with the coffees.

"I couldn't help myself," Amy laughed.

"How does it feel to be back?"

"How does it feel to still be here?" I asked.

"You first."

"Surreal. Nice. Sad."

"Sad?"

"Things never got better," I said.

"That could have been D-Ream's follow-up song for Tony Blair," Ed joked.

Amy and Ed noticed that I wasn't joking.

"You've got to change your perspective a little," Ed said. "I'm the worst fucking teacher in the world, and I wake up every single day thinking that today will be the day they realise, and I'll be an unemployed ex-raver who took far too many disco biscuits between 1987 and 1992. But I get through it, because I know that if it all ended tomorrow, it would mean nothing in the grand scheme of things. Life goes on."

Amy wiped out the word 'BALL BAG' and changed it to 'LEGEND'. I laughed, and Ed tapped my coffee mug with his.

"You're twenty-three years old with no commitments and a pretty face. Get out there and get some life experience, man. If this was the pinnacle of your life so far, you've got to make an effort to blow it out of the water so it becomes a footnote."

I could see why Ed had become course leader, and why the powers-that-be would never get rid of him; he was a lovely, lovely guy, and easily the most positive person I'd ever met.

He was right, too. Time to see old memories for what they were: old memories. And replace them with new ones. Better ones. New laughs, new mistakes, new challenges. New everything.

Amy and I looked back at our old haunt as we left.

"I used to love coming here every day," I said.

"Me too."

"Does it make me sad? The fact that I haven't moved on?"

"Not at all. But at least with the wedding – and coming home – you've got the chance to do that."

Amy and I agreed to meet in a few days to go shopping in Leicester for a wedding gift. When I told her that we would be accompanied by Jim and Sean – and the fact that I was living with them both – she burst out laughing. It was suddenly all so clear, she said. It wasn't just the dream of Lila Holmes that had chained me to the past. Amy had done exactly the same thing, but at least she was marrying her housemate. I just played Xbox, watched films and talked about disgusting things with mine, and it suddenly didn't seem as cool as it used to. I'd used them to hold on to the best years of my life, and they'd used me for cheaper rent and/or to get over a break-up. It was time for a change. Australia started to sound like a realistic option after all.

I laid in bed that night thinking about how I would break it to Sean and Jim that I was leaving. Being the kind of person who thinks about things to the point where his entire life stands still, I saw about one thousand scenarios, some of which included ninja weapons and explosions, others where The Lonely Man theme from *The Incredible Hulk* played over a slow-motion walk into the sunset. I came to the conclusion that I would break it to them gently once the wedding was out of the way.

By the time I'd worked all of this out, my bladder was full to bursting. There's nothing worse than being at the point of sleep but also needing the toilet. I closed my eyes and hoped the feeling would subside, but I'd waited too long. Fuckle-Doodle-Doo.

As I crept out of my old bedroom and onto the landing, I noticed that the TV was on downstairs. Against my better judgement, I decided to investigate instead of going for a pee.

I put the pain to one side and crept downstairs. I used to sneak downstairs to nick biscuits in the middle of the night when I was little, hence the memorising of the creaking steps. It also explained my love for biscuits. Hmm, biscuits...

Dad was sitting in his chair, still dressed, nodding in and out of sleep. The music video for 'Ironic' by Alanis Morissette was playing on the TV, and the clock read 2:42am.

I approached him slowly, and he turned to me and smiled.

"Hey. Can't sleep?" he asked.

"What are you doing?"

"Watching TV."

"I can see that. Why?"

"I fell asleep down here. It's not a big deal."

"It is a big deal when I've already picked up on the fact that you're hardly looking at each other, let alone talking. And now I've found you here..."

Dad sighed, and sat upright in his chair.

"Don't worry about us, son. We'll be alright."

"Mum isn't alright, Dad. She's been hit really hard by this thing. You need to grow a pair and look after her. She needs you."

I could feel myself filling up with rage. All the things I wish I'd said but kept quiet. All the things I wish I'd done but did nothing. All the places I wish I'd been but I stayed in the same place. It was all bubbling to the surface, and Dad was getting the brunt of it.

"I've been punishing myself every day since being invited to this wedding. I'm a fucking failure, I know that now. But I'm not going to be anymore. And I'm not going to let you become one either by failing with Mum."

Dad could see that I was furious. He put his hand up to me to calm me down, as my voice was starting to rise.

"I'm struggling with her illness, Jay. Some people cope with things better than others. I don't know what to say, what to do. It's hard for me, too."

"That's great, but ignoring her and letting her wait on you doesn't help either. It's better to make an effort and be left feeling like a dick than to not make an effort at all."

"You're right, you're right. I'm sorry."

"Then stop sitting down here watching four Alanis Morissette's singing in a fucking car and go and hold your wife, who is sleeping alone right now."

I had only ever seen dad cry once, and that was when Stuart Pearce missed his penalty against West Germany in 1990, and was consoled by Chris Waddle. It was only a tear, but it still counts. A tear rolled down his cheek for the first time since that day, and it made me gasp when I spotted it.

"I know that part of the blame lies with me. I didn't want to get involved with her business. It was her baby. I didn't step back and say 'I told you so', but I guess I didn't do enough either."

"Its emotional support she needs right now, not financial."

Dad nodded his head about a thousand times before getting to his feet and lunging towards me. He put his arms around me and pulled me close to him. I gave him a firm, manly slap on the back. What I really wanted to do was cry like a big wet baby.

Dad pulled me from him and held me in place so he could take a good long look at the weird biological experiment that was his only son.

"You've turned out alright," he said, smiling.

"I just want both of you to be happy. I don't want to worry about you."

"Don't worry. Now give me a kiss."

"Your face is like a bear's arsehole."

Dad chuckled and gave me another hug.

It was a sweet moment.

But I needed a piss so bad.

10. Plus One, Twice, Three Times the Lady

A text came through at 9:17am the next morning:

"MORNING FUCK NUGGET, JIM AND I HAVE SET YOU WITH TWO DATES IN ONE DAY. STARTING AT 3PM. YOU CAN THANK US AFTER YOU WET YOUR WILLY. LOVE SEAN XXX"

Two dates in one day? How was that supposed to work? I texted back that I was grateful and more than a little terrified. Sean texted me again, "3PM. DMU LEISURE CENTRE. JIM WILL BRING YOUR GYM GEAR."

I thought back to the two girls that Jim and Sean had mentioned setting me up with: Toni the nineteen-year-old Army cadet/fitness fanatic, and Tina the twenty-year-old tomboy who worked with Sean. I figured that I should go for the hat trick and set up a date with Helen, so I texted her from my bed.

"HI HELEN, ITS JASON. THE GUY FROM THE BEECH TREE WHO YOU GAVE YOUR BUSINESS CARD TO. I SURVIVED. FANCY DOING SOMETHING TOMORROW?"

Within seconds, a reply came in.

"I DON'T KNOW A JASON."

Fuck.

The phone vibrated with another message.

"JUST KIDDING. GLAD TO HEAR YOU SURVIVED. SURE, LET'S MEET UP FOR A DRINK. WHEN WERE YOU THINKING? I'M FREE TOMORROW…"

I texted back.

"SOUNDS PERFECT."

"MEET ME AT THE SCENE OF OUR INTRODUCTION AT SIX?"

Boom. It was a date. Three dates, to be exact. The first in a long time, too. No pressure. Lots of pressure. Too much pressure. Time to take the toaster to the bath with me.

Once I'd calmed down, refreshed myself and munched on some cereal, the dates seemed like a great idea. The odds were in my favour that I would make at least a good enough impression to get a plus one for the wedding, unless they asked me to carry trays to the kitchen.

I had a cup of tea with mum and told her the good news. She thought I was a tart.

"Three dates?" she said. "I dated one person before I met your dad."

"Ah, the one that got away," I joked.

"He's bald as a coot and fatter than your father is now. Lucky escape."

It was good to see mum in better spirits.

"I'm going to go back today and see how these dates go. I'll be back again in a few days, and we'll spend some proper time together. OK?"

"Sounds perfect," said Mum, smiling like she was already looking forward to it.

"When Dad gets back from work, tell him that his son has three dates. That'll show him who the lady killer is in the family."

"I'll tell him. Not sure his heart will take it though."

I arrived back in Leicester at 11:52, and immediately realised that I was stupidly early. Fortunately, the HMV sale was on. It didn't matter how bored I was, or how much time I had to kill, I could always use HMV to run down the clock. I would either search for classics, look for the worst film I could possibly find (and buy it for Jim) or go through the TV box sets for shows that I loved as a kid. I bought series one and two of *Brush Strokes* the last time I was there. I loved that show.

By the time I had gone through the sales, it was time to go to the leisure centre. And yes, that means I spent three hours looking at DVD's. Go ahead and judge me. The truth was, I was so nervous, I just stared at the covers whilst trembling in fear over the fact that we were meeting at the gym. Do people really do that? Were we going to run alongside each other on the treadmill and get to know each other that way? I was hardly at the peak of my physical powers, so anything more than five sit-ups and a wheatgrass smoothie was unlikely to serve me well on a first date.

Within a couple of minutes of my arrival, Jim came towards me holding a gym bag. He was accompanied by a tall, beautiful blonde-haired girl with a cute face and the longest, leanest legs I'd ever seen. Instantly, I knew that I was in trouble. Jim – professional liar and utter bastard – had probably told her I'd run the London Marathon without breaking a sweat and farted in Seb Coe's face as I breezed past him.

Jim threw me the gym bag and introduced me to his friend.

"Numb nuts, this is Toni. Toni, this is Jason. My best friend."

"Hi," I said, and shook Toni's hand. "I hope you haven't listened to a word he's told you about me."

"Now I'm worried. He's only told me nice things."

Oops.

"I hope you don't mind spinning with me. This was the only time I had available for the next few weeks. I'm going away tomorrow. Is that cool?"

Spinning? What the fuck was spinning? Were we going into the mind of Pete Burns? I couldn't ask. I pretended to know something about physical activities instead.

"Spinning sounds great. I hope Jim has packed shorts and T-shirt for me, and not his Spiderman outfit."

A puzzled Toni turned to Jim for an explanation, and Jim panicked. It was the first time I'd managed to rattle him for a long time. It was always the other way around.

"Err, yeah… I'm a Marvel collector. I'll see you guys later."

Jim stepped away, mouthing the word "motherfucker" to me as he left us to enter the realm of almost certain death.

"Shall we get ready for spinning?" Toni asked, leaning towards the entrance of the gym.

"Let's spin!" I said, with all the excitement I could muster.

The male changing room was a box, and smelt like a pair of socks that hadn't been washed in 240 years. The air was a mix of stale Lynx and body odour, and all the men felt the need to walk around with their tackle on show, coughing every four seconds.

I made the point of turning around so nobody could see my donger. I'm a grower, not a shower, and some of those guys were hung like fire hoses. One guy – who looked like one of the Goons from Popeye – could easily have slung his warrior over his shoulder and worn it as a fashion accessory. I wanted to shake his hand and congratulate him on his achievement.

I met Toni upstairs. She was wearing a pair of black shorts that were smaller than my boxers and the tightest white vest I'd ever seen. Even with no make-up and her hair tied back she looked awesome, and more than a little intimidating. Every time she moved, I could see the muscles working. I predicted 13% body fat, which made me realise that I didn't sleep through the Sports Science module of my Leisure and Tourism course.

"Ready to rock?" Toni asked.

"Sure am," I replied, sucking my gut in as much as possible.

Toni entered a small dark room that was next to the main section of the gym, and I dutifully followed. The room was filled with manual exercise bikes, and when she jumped onto a bike at the front of the room, I smiled with relief.

Spinning is bike riding? Piece of piss.

I jumped on the bike, and Toni and I shared a smile.

"It's 45 minutes, pretty intense. But nothing you can't handle," Toni said, reassuringly.

"Cool."

"Then we'll grab a coffee downstairs, yeah?"

"Perfect!"

More people entered the room, all of them as toned and athletic as Toni. My BMI was fairly normal, but I looked morbidly obese next to these guys. And then the instructor came in. Remember Shadow from Gladiators? Imagine if he'd moved to Leicester and ditched his spandex and giant cotton buds for Nike.

He clapped his hands together a few times, as if to psyche himself up, and I glanced over at Toni and then around the room at the other people taking part in the class. They were deadly silent, composed and taking deep breaths in preparation. It dawned on me that I was about to cough my spleen out of my mouth.

Shadow MKII put on the loudest dance music you'll hear outside of Creamfields and started to dance in front of the class. Then he started chanting.

"Move! Move! Move! Move! Move! Move! Move!"

The class started biking, and biking fast. I started too, and within seconds, Shadow was onto me.

"Welcome to the parrrrrrrrrrrrr-tay!" he screamed at me.

"Non-stopping, just keep rocking!" he shouted, and started flinging his arms around.

The class were mimicking what he was doing with his dance moves, and it all started to make sense. I thought he was some crackhead who fancied a party with some cyclists and had sneaked past reception. I joined in the best I could, but within a couple of minutes I was blowing out of my arse and sweating profusely.

Ten minutes in, and Shadow held his arms out in front of him and started bobbing up and down. The class mimicked this, lifting their arses from their seats and putting their arms out in front of them.

It's difficult to do all of this whilst you're peddling like you're escaping a rapist, and my thighs were burning like hell. If Toni hadn't been there, I would have run for my life by now.

I started to find my groove about twenty minutes in. It would've been lovely for someone to bring in some spare boxer shorts at this point, because mine had collected a pint of sweat that could have a water-balloon fight effect if I suddenly sat down. Toni would be really turned on by the sight of me covering the man behind me in ball soup.

Shadow clearly loved the underdog. He kept running up to me and shouting 'GO! GO! GO! GO!' and 'HELLLLLLLL YEAAAAAAAAAAAH!' in my face to make me go faster, and to be fair to him, it worked. I couldn't believe that I was still alive, let alone still able to keep up with the class, albeit in a far sweatier, much slower capacity.

I glanced over at Toni. She had a light glistening on her forehead and a little blushing on her cheeks, but other than that, she looked like a fitness-wear model. She was breathing in through her nose, out via her mouth and staring forward at Shadow. I was praying for a quick death and breathing like someone was repeatedly punching me in the gut.

At the 45 minute mark, Shadow jumped in the air and shouted "Cooooooool dowwwwwwwwwn!" Everybody in the room sat upright and slowed their peddling down to a crawl, and Shadow turned the music down to a reasonable volume.

After a few minutes cool down, Shadow turned the lights up to their full brightness and hit 'stop' on the music player.

"That's it, champs. Well done. You've done yourselves proud," he said.

The class started to dismount their bikes and leave. Toni swung her incredibly toned left leg over her bike and stepped off her perch to greet me.

My head was buried in my handle bars, and my asshole felt like Mike Tyson had used it as a punch bag for 45 minutes.

A concerned Toni and Shadow came over to me.

"Are you okay, Jason?" Toni asked.

"Brother, you should be proud of yourself," Shadow said in a voice that was deeper than Barry White, only in a South Leicester accent rather than South Central LA.

"Thanks," I replied. "I'm scared to move."

"I thought you were some dick who had turned up thinking this class would be a doddle. You stayed firm and kept at it. You've earned my respect."

Even though I thought my arsehole was about to explode, I couldn't help but feel proud listening to Shadow's words of encouragement.

"Thank you, sir." I whimpered.

"Call me Clive."

I will call you Shadow, Clive. And I will never see you again.

"Are you ready to grab that coffee?" asked Toni.

"Yes," I replied.

I pushed myself gently off my seat and stood upright.

"I think I'm good to walk," I said, and attempted to move my left leg forward.

Being caught and cradled back to consciousness by a huge black man was not the ideal way to endear myself to Toni, but we agreed to meet up in the café area of the gym once we had got showered and changed, which took me a lot longer to achieve than Toni.

It felt weird to pay for an espresso for a change, but I would've sold my arse for a cup of the brown stuff, if my arse wasn't throbbing like Mick Jagger's lips after 12 rounds with a prime Naseem Hamed.

I shuffled up to the table where Toni was waiting for me. She smiled as I lowered myself slowly into my seat.

"Bless you… I thought you knew what you were getting in for," she said.

"How does somebody get fit enough to do that without dying?"

"Hard work and dedication."

"Yeah… I don't have either of those attributes."

"Clive was right though. You could have given up and left. You did really well to stick it out to the end. You're stronger and more competitive than you realise."

My phone vibrated in my pocket. I pulled it out and checked it. It was Sean.

"TINA IS GOING TO MEET YOU AT 7PM AT THE WHITE HOUSE. SHE'S GOT A PIC OF YOU SO DON'T WORRY. SHE'S A BOOZE HOUND SO BE CAREFUL. HAHA. SEE YOU LATER. SEAN XXX"

I could have slept for a thousand years. The idea of talking to people in a social environment had lost its appeal. I put my phone away and sipped my coffee. I stared forward for a few moments and felt my legs slowly seizing up. Toni broke me out of my daydream by giggling.

"Wow, I've really tired you out," she said.

"I'm sorry. I'm being so rude."

"Not at all. I wish we were at my place. I could lay you out on the sofa and nurse you back to health."

"That sounds like a fantastic idea!"

"Unfortunately," she said.

That word is never followed by anything good.

"I have to go shortly. But I'd love to see you again sometime. Maybe in a less physical environment?"

"Definitely in a less physical environment," I agreed.

I looked like an eighty-year-old billionaire escorting my gold digger wife around as we left the gym, and Toni gave me a kiss on the cheek as she prepared to leave.

"You have my number. Give me a call in a few weeks?"

"That's optimistic. I'll be at the chiropractor's for a month."

Toni laughed.

"You'll be fine. Have an ice bath. They're amazing. I'll see you."

"See you."

Any girl – regardless of how beautiful – who takes ice baths after a gym session is never going to be the right fit for a person whose idea of an ice bath was a double Jack Daniels, and for whom physical activity was walking from the bed to the sofa. Toni was on a different level to me, and deserved someone who could match Clive for fitness rather than testing his ability to catch fainters. It was worth the pain to watch her walk away though. Damn.

I killed the sixty minutes before meeting Tina at the White House by shuffling down the High Street at 0.5 miles an hour. Sean had described Tina as a tomboy and a boozer who is always up for a laugh. Right now, I wasn't in a fit enough state to have a cup of tea at my Nan's house. My body ached and I was carrying a gym bag filled with clothes that would stick to the wall if you threw them at it.

I heard my name being called from one of the tables in the far corner as I entered the pub. I gazed over and saw Tina, barely five feet tall and mousey with cropped brown hair, waving for me to come over. She was wearing black jeans and a blue hoodie.

I couldn't have picked two more contrasting dates, but the fact that Tina had two empty pint glasses on her table convinced me that Clive wasn't going to dive through the window at any minute holding two bikes and screaming "Surprise motherfucker! Now… Mooooooove!"

Tina held out her hand as I approached.

"Hey Tina, I'm Jason," I said, grimacing through the thigh pain.

"What's with the formal stuff?" she said, and gave me a hug instead.

"I'll get the beers in, shall I? You sit down. Sean told me that you've just come from a spinning class. Your arse must be banging."

Tina was forward, but it was welcomed. She wandered off to the bar and I plonked myself on a stool. I had a feeling that this night could get messy, and I was more than up for that after the horror show at the gym.

Tina came back from the bar and sat down with two pints.

"Drinking pints. I like your style," I said.

"I'm just too fucking lazy to keep going to the bar," she laughed, before putting her hand to her mouth. "I'm really sorry. I swear a lot."

"It's fine," I said. "You're friends with Sean."

"He's been singing your praises. He told me you're very fragile and that I should go easy on you… Not in that way, obviously."

I liked this girl. She was nuttier than a squirrels shit.

We had a few drinks and talked about Lila, the wedding, how much of a dick Sean was and all kinds of other stuff. After about four pints, my body reacted like I'd been hooked up to an Aftershock drip.

Intense physical activity + beer = Holy fuck.

The last time alcohol hit me suddenly I woke up covered in rice and with no chance of a second date. I finished my drink and looked at Tina who – in my inebriated state – had split into three people.

"Uh-oh, someone's a lightweight."

"I think it's the spinning class. It's sped up my meta-meta-metabo-lism…"

"Nah. You're just pissed. Let's go to mine."

Tina grabbed my arm and launched me out of my seat. I managed to grab my bag of sweat-drenched rags before being thrown out of the pub and into the street.

Before I had a chance to speak, Tina has shoved her tongue down my throat, and cupped my pain-stricken butt cheeks with her hands. My lack of practice meant that I had absolutely no penis control, and the little lad had recovered from the horrors of the male changing room and was rising to Tina's forward-thinking. As soon as I realised this, I put my hand down the front of my jeans and put my friend to 12 o'clock. This – as every man knows – would keep him from embarrassing me in the event that any passers-by looked south.

I had won the Battle of the Bulge, and soon enough, Tina was starting to fumble for her house keys. She must've had a built-in sat nav in her head, because we'd spent the last twenty minutes wading through the city streets with our faces meshed together and our eyes closed.

Tina broke free of my mouth and jogged up the steps of a three-storey house that had been converted into flats. I followed her to the door as she unlocked it, and kissed her neck as she broke some news to me.

"I should tell you, I don't live alone," she said.

"That's cool. I don't either."

"As long as you're OK with that."

At this point, she could be living with Clive and the entire cast of the Gladiators and I wouldn't care. I was starting to lose the Battle of the Bulge and the door couldn't open fast enough.

Tina and I came crashing through the main doors of the house and then through the door of her first-floor flat. Turned out that the house had been converted into bedsits, and Tina was sharing with a stoner couple who had fallen asleep with a joint on.

Two words: fire risk.

The room was essentially a sink, a desk, a wardrobe, two posters comprising of the Bob Marley "Legend" LP cover and Reservoir Dogs, and two mattresses pushed together.

I stood open mouthed at the door, staring at the two woolly-jumper wearing stoners snoring into each other's faces whilst cradling each other.

"I didn't think they'd be here," Tina said, taking her hoodie off and throwing it onto a desk filled with pizza and cigarette boxes.

"Are you still up for this? They won't wake up. You could kick them in the face and they wouldn't shift. Look."

Tina pushed her foot against the guys back. He groaned, then started snoring.

"Erm…"

Every fibre of my being wanted to leave. Except my penis. He wanted to stay. And he always wins.

I launched myself at Tina, and we shed each other's clothes as we crawled onto the mattress next to the snoring stoners whilst attempting to eat each other's faces. It was every shade of wrong, and it was pretty fucking exciting.

I managed to hook Tina's duvet onto my foot and fling it over us. She grabbed it and wrapped it around us, before her hand crept inside to grab my friend. Her hands were freezing, but neither I nor my buddy were bothered. She felt me up for a while, but foreplay was the furthest thing from both our minds, and I entered her as quickly as I could.

I had waited a long time for this moment, and part of me expected it to be over so fast that it would be classed as negative time. Fortunately, the numbness and pain that the spinning class had inflicted on me was helping me last longer than I had any right to expect.

Tina made eye contact with me and smiled, which was nice, as it took my attention away from the sweaty yeti spooning his girlfriend beside me, who I was desperate not to wake up. After a few moments, we both allowed ourselves to close our eyes and enjoy it.

I started to think about Toni in those shorts.

Bad idea.

How about Clive in those shorts?

That's better.

One day, aliens will do studies on how we procreate and come to the conclusion that we are seriously fucking strange and leave the planet pronto.

Tina started to make noise, and I liked it. I upped the tempo as the finishing line came into sight, and as I approached the home straight, I gazed to my left and pulled my best sex face, which was a one-eyed squint that made me look like Popeye after a horse tranquilliser.

Unfortunately, my one opened eye noticed that the man sleeping next to us was now very much awake, was watching us, and had now seen my sex face.

"Keep going, man. Don't mind me. I'm not even here," he whispered, and turned his back to us.

I was filled with a mixture of horror and disgust, but before it could put off the old friend downstairs, Tina dug her nails into my back and pulled me closer to her, and all morals and self-respect went out of the window.

I finished, and instantly felt the shame wash over me.

Tina stroked my hair and looked into my eyes.

"Are you sleeping here? You can if you like," she whispered, as if the bearded freak to our left wasn't awake and listening to every word.

"I can't. I've got an early start. I'm in no rush though."

"I can see that," she said, a mischievous smile growing on her face.

I rolled onto my back and Tina snuggled into me. It would have been perfect, had I not been face-to-face with a Sasquatch five seconds before the grand finale. A Sasquatch that was now close enough that I could feel the wool from his jumper on my arm.

Tina managed to sneak me out of her flat three hours later, and I took the walk of shame home. I sniggered to myself at how disgusting I had been, but there was a part of me that was a little bit pleased with myself. I now had a sex story to tell people in pubs. This was what I was missing out on, and it was something I could get used to. Minus the hairy stoners, of course.

11. Emotional Maturity

Remember the scene in *Wayne's World 2* where Garth loses his virginity to Kim Basinger and enters the room the next day smoking a pipe, wearing a jacket and talking like a distinguished gent?

That's how I felt the morning after my strange-yet-fun evening with Tina.

My entire body had seized up from the spinning sessions, but it was worth it. As I came down the stairs, Sean peeped around the kitchen door with an expectant smile on his face.

"Hey buddy, how did last night go?"

"Very well, thank you," I said, wearing the smuggest grin on my face.

"Ah, it went that well, did it? Nice work. Details?"

"A gentleman doesn't kiss and tell."

"Exactly. Details?"

I laughed and joined Sean in the kitchen, who to my surprise was making himself poached eggs on toast.

"What the fuck? Are you eating healthily now?" I asked.

"Yeah man, the wedding is coming up. Gotta get in shape."

"I don't mean to be a dick, but the wedding is two weeks away."

"I take your point. I started a little late... Do you want some?"

"I'll stick to Shreddies, buddy. I haven't been a fan of cooked breakfasts since the whole 'getting fired' thing..."

Sean chuckled and dished out his poached eggs, arranging them artistically on his toast like he was presenting them to Marcus Wareing.

"Can I ask a question?" Sean asked.

"Sure."

"Why are you walking like the guy from *Reach for the Sky*?"

"Did you not hear about my spinning class with Toni? I've been texting Jim abusive messages for the last 12 hours."

"Spinning class? Fucking sadist."

"I know, right? I'm going to be stiff for weeks."

"Tina's fun, right?"

"Yeah she was cool. We had a laugh. Just what I needed. Someone who would have a giggle and a drink. It was fun."

"Good to hear it. Is she going to be your plus one? I've got a £10 bet with Jim that you'd pick her. He wins if you take Toni. Don't let him win. He did try and kill you with a manual exercise bike."

"Neither of you are winning. I'm meeting up with Helen later. Y'know, the lady we met at The Beech Tree?"

Sean wracked his brain.

"The MILF?"

I rolled my eyes and sighed.

"Yes, the MILF."

"Don't come over all Feminist of the Year with me, you whopper."

I laughed and helped myself to Shreddies.

I spent most of the day thinking of ways to tell Jim and Sean that I would be moving out. Stuff like changing the lease, packing my stuff and actually working out what the hell I was going to do once I had moved out were running through my mind, and it quickly dawned on me that I had a lot of work to do.

Amy text me to see when I was free to go wedding list shopping. I told her that I was free anytime, and that I'd check with Sean and Jim to see when they were free. Fortunately, they were both in the position that they could pretty much work whenever they wanted, as long as they completed their 40 hours a week.

I arranged a Thursday afternoon meet up, for no other reason than the fact that I couldn't bear to go shopping at the weekend. George A Romero hit the nail on the head with *Dawn on the Dead*. As soon as humans step inside a bright shopping centre, hear plinkety plink music and stand on escalators, they're doomed to walk the earth as the undead. I don't have the patience for that.

I sat at my computer desk for around five hours, looking at pictures of Australia and trying to figure out the working visa situation. It was surprisingly less migraine inducing than I thought it would be, and using the travel website, ordered my visa and priced up a return trip from London Heathrow to Brisbane 365 days apart. I had to wait a while to see if the visa application would be approved, which gave me time to break it to the guys and my parents.

Everything was coming together nicely.

The clock hit 5pm and I jumped in the shower to get ready for my date with Helen. For the first time in my dating life, I gave serious thought to what I was going to wear, and opted for smarter gear than I'd usually throw on. The majority of my smart clothes still had the creases in them from where I'd taken them out of the bag the shop had packaged them in and never touched them again.

Whenever I had an "I'm going to make more of an effort" epiphany, the first course of action would always be to spend some money on nice clothes I'd never wear. Now was the time to give them an airing. Helen didn't want to go on a date with a kid in jeans and a Nike T-shirt. She was a classy career woman ten years my senior. I had to up my game.

I opted for my brown Italian moleskin trousers, black shoes – nicely shined, I might add – and a blue and black Armani shirt that I purchased in 1998, wore once and never again. Until today. The fact that it still fitted me filled me with confidence.

Helen was sitting in the outside seating area of the pub when I arrived, and was seated under the glow of the heated lamps and looked pretty fucking spectacular in a figure-hugging black dress, and more than a little intimidating to a guy who spent last night having sex with a twenty-year-old part-time student next to a hairy guy. A sophisticated woman was going to see through this underachieving man-child within seconds and leave.

Helen greeted me with a kiss on both cheeks, something that I'd only experienced from the comfort of my sofa while watching the Oscars in my joggers.

"How are you doing? Have you recovered from the last time I saw you?" Helen asked.

"I have indeed. You look amazing, by the way."

"Thank you. I hope you don't mind, but I ordered us some wine?"

One of the bar staff brought over a bottle of wine and two glasses.

"Not at all," I said.

"You're still at the age when hangovers last for minutes and not days. Wait until you're on the wrong side of thirty. They're killers."

The server poured us two glasses of wine and placed the bottle into the ice. We both thanked him and took a sip. I tried hard not to pull my disgusted face, as the wine was disgusting. But I was prepared to take one in the name of making a positive impression.

"You're not really selling me on the idea of post-thirty life," I joked.

"Oh, it's great. I wasn't saying that. The hangovers hurt more, but everything else is fantastic. You have more confidence, you don't second guess yourself, and you don't suffer fools."

"Wow. That sounds awesome. I live with two fools, I'm constantly second guessing myself and my confidence… well, that's a series of peaks and troughs."

"Yep. Sounds like twenties," Helen said.

I felt at ease with Helen, but there was a nagging feeling in the back of my mind that she was already struggling for anything to talk about other than the age difference. It wasn't helped by the fact that she met me whilst out on a self-destructive binge drinking session. I figured that I would try and steer the conversation to her and her life, in a bid to disguise the fact that I was twenty-three going on fifteen.

"Tell me about you. What do you do for fun? I've read your business card, I know you work in recruitment. What else should I know?"

"Well, here goes. The short list… I am divorced, I have an eight-year-old daughter named Molly, and now you are instantly regretting asking me that question."

I bolted upright in my chair.

"What? No way," I said, defensively.

"I thought I would throw those two things out there to test you. To be fair, you passed. I've been on dates where the guy has started checking his watch or made excuses to leave as soon as I mentioned my daughter."

"Not at all. I love kids. I used to be one. I went to a school filled with the buggers."

Helen laughed and loosened up a little. She stroked her shin with her right hand and it took all of my self-control not to watch her do it. I used my peripheral vision to avoid looking like a perv, and took a sip of my rank wine to take my attention away from her leg.

"She's a beautiful little girl," she said, proudly.

"I'm sure she is. Is your ex-husband still in her life?"

"Yes. Very much so. Harry's a good guy, it just didn't work out. You know?"

"Sure. It's nice that he's still there for Molly, though."

"Definitely."

The triviality of my own issues hit me like a speeding train. Here was a beautiful, successful, single-mother who had the dignity not to slag off her ex to me and maintain a friendship with him for the sake of her daughter, and my entire life had been turned upside down because I'd been invited to a fucking wedding?

We chatted over wine for about an hour, and for the most part, the conversation flowed nicely. I asked about Molly and what she was like, and Helen asked me how I ended up living with Jim and Sean, which she found hilarious. She made an excellent observation, too: you hardly ever hear of girls living together outside of uni digs. They usually live alone, with parents or with a partner. It was mostly guys who moved in together and enjoyed a group therapy session that consisted of beer, processed food and rock hard socks. Blame *Fight Club*.

Just as we were getting into a relaxed rhythm, Helen's phone rang, and she stood up and moved away as she spoke to whoever was on the other end. I took the opportunity to finish off the horrendous wine and turned the bottle upside down in the ice bucket. Good riddance, you disgusting grape-piss fusion.

Helen came back to the table and apologised for having to answer the phone, and the anticipation of an excuse to leave crept over me. I assumed that she had told a friend to call her after an hour so that she could escape.

"I'm so sorry to do this, but I've got to run. My babysitter's got a family emergency to deal with, and my folks are on holiday so I don't have anyone else. I'm going to have to run."

In my eagerness to be a negative prick, I wanted to stand up and applaud the performance. But sometimes you need to believe that people are genuine.

"Why don't you come with me? You could meet Molly? Only if you like…"

Helen was 100% expecting me to run for my life at this moment, but I was enjoying her company and I figured that it was time to show that I had at least a smidgeon of emotional maturity.

"Sure, I'd love to," I said.

"Great."

We jumped in a taxi and headed back to Helen's house, which was a modern four-bedroomed detached house in the Stoneygate area of Leicester. I had always wanted to move to that end of town, but that dream died the second I read the rental rates.

You know you've gone up in the world when you walk into a house and instantly want to take your shoes off. Most people walked into my house and put wellingtons on. I took my shoes off and followed Helen through to the living room, where a cute little girl was waiting for her mum.

"Hi Molls," said Helen.

Molly gripped her mum around the waist and looked up at her.

"Can I have a banana milkshake?" She asked.

"Good question. Why don't you ask my new friend Jason if he would like one, too?"

Helen swung Molly around to face me. Molly looked at me with cautious eyes.

"I would love a banana milkshake, and I'm very happy to meet you, Molly."

I approached Molly and put out my hand to shake it. Molly put out her fist instead.

"She's more of a 'fist bump' girl," said Helen.

"Me too. We have so much in common."

I gave Molly a fist bump and she seemed to warm to me a little. Then came the awkwardness that only kids can provide.

"Is Jason your boyfriend?" she asked.

Helen turned to me and we both burst into embarrassed laughter.

"Let's just say he's my friend, who happens to be a boy?"

Good save, mum.

Molly turned her nose up at that one. At that age, she probably had about a hundred boyfriends, or friends that happened to be boys. Fed up with the grown up conversation and wanting a milkshake, Molly jumped on the sofa and started playing a Game Boy Advance. Helen dealt with the departing babysitter and took charge of the milkshake situation.

"Go and sit down," she said.

I took a seat on the sofa across from Molly. Molly didn't look up from the Game Boy, and I decided not to force the conversation and put her off her game. But then, I felt a shiver of joy flow up my spine as I recognised the beloved tones of Super Mario World.

I had been the ultimate Mario geek, having owned every Mario game from 1985 to 2002. For the first time in my adult life, I had something to say to a child other than "How's school?"

"Which world are you on?" I asked.

Molly looked at me over the top of the Game Boy.

"Chocolate Island," she replied.

I could tell that she was unsure of why I was asking questions about Mario.

"Have you been to the Star World yet?" I asked.

Molly sighed.

"Yes. But it's hard."

"It is hard. It is."

Molly continued playing, but her eyes kept looking up at me and back to the screen. After a few moments, she paused the game and came and sat next to me. She passed me the Game Boy and shuffled up next to me. I moved away at first, but she was going to be follow me everywhere, so I stayed still and took the Game Boy from her. Personal space means nothing when you're a precocious kid.

"Can you show me?" Molly asked.

"Of course. I've completed all 96 levels on this game. I am Mario!"

Molly mouthed the word 'geek' and her eyes glued to the screen as I went about my Mario mission. I went back through the levels to find the Star World level that Molly had struggled with. I was ten years old again.

Helen came back into the room holding a tray with three banana milkshakes on it. She smiled when she saw two children beating Mario World together and put the tray down on the coffee table in front of us. I looked up from the Game Boy and smiled to say thanks. Molly didn't even look up. She was engrossed. Is making friends with kids always this easy?

"I think it's time for Mario to take a break and Molly to have a banana milkshake before bed," Helen said.

Molly sighed and resigned herself to a Mario-less evening. I paused the game and handed her the Game Boy, and she packed it away before drinking her milkshake.

I moved forward to the edge of the sofa. I thought that I would be a gentleman and see myself out.

Helen picked Molly up. They were a great match.

"Say goodnight to Jason," said Helen.

"Goodnight to Jason," said Molly.

"Ha-ha-ha, you are hilarious!"

Molly laughed and gave me a wave as Helen took her upstairs to bed.

I stood up to make my way to the front door, but before I got out of the living room, my phone vibrated.

"GIVE ME FIVE MINUTES WITH YOUR NEW BUDDY AND I'LL BE WITH YOU. DON'T RUN FOR THE EXIT!! H XXX"

I sat back down on the sofa. I was surprisingly relaxed for someone who had never dated someone over my own age, let alone someone with actual life experience, an ex-husband and a cute small person to care for. But when I thought about it, this was all I ever wanted for myself. I played the field about as comfortably as a blind centre forward plays an FA Cup final. All I wanted was the comfort of a solid relationship, I just hadn't been ready for one until now.

I still had work to do.

Helen came back into the living room and I stood up to greet her. She walked up to me slowly and stood right in front of me. I closed my eyes and leaned in to kiss her. This was a different kind of kiss to the face-eating competition I had participated in with Tina 24 hours previously. There was a depth of feeling to this one that gave me chills.

Helen leaned back from me and smiled.

"You were extremely cute sitting on the sofa with Molly," she said.

"Making friends with children is easy when they have Mario and you are the same school age."

Helen laughed and kissed me again.

"You don't have to leave yet, do you? I've made milkshakes."

"That all depends on how good your milkshakes are. Do they bring all the boys to the yard?"

"Yup."

"In that case, it would be rude not to stay."

Helen smiled and we sat down on the sofa with our milkshakes, which were – for the record – pretty fucking good, especially when followed up with banana flavoured kisses.

When the kisses went up a notch on the passion meter, Helen pulled away.

"I should tell you… I'm not going to sleep with you tonight."

I nodded in agreement, even though I was devastated by the news. The devastation then turned to guilt when I realised that Helen was annoyed with herself for ruining the moment.

"I'm sorry. There was no need to say that," she said.

"It's fine. Honestly. Whatever you want to do, I'm OK with it."

Helen looked into my eyes and smiled.

"Are you cut out for doing this again?" she asked.

"Erm, yes, at least if you want to?"

"Yeah, why not? You're funny."

"Thanks?" I said, in the hope that at least another five compliments were to follow.

"I hope you don't mind me saying this… But I saw something in you that day when your friend introduced us… A sadness."

I shuffled uncomfortably in my seat, and tried to deflect the comment with humour.

"Wow, this is getting deep…"

"I'm sorry."

"No, no, no… it's fine. You're right. There is sadness there. Definitely."

Helen gently stroked my hair, and as I looked at her, I felt like she was 100% genuine, cared for me, and that I wanted to pour every ounce of truth out onto the table in front of her.

"I received an invite to the wedding of my first, well, only, love. And it made me realise how pathetic I've been in the past five years. Living with my two best friends to make me feel good about myself, and working as many hours as I can, so I don't have the time to sit back and realise what a failure I am."

Helen gave me a sympathetic smile and took our milkshakes away so that we could get closer to each other. She put her head against mine and placed her hands either side of my face.

"I understand how you're feeling. When Harry left me I thought that everyone looked at me like a typical single mum. A benefits cheat with nothing to offer the world. But I worked my arse off to make our relationship work enough for Molly not to suffer, and so I could work hard and achieve what I wanted to achieve. It's easier to fall into apathy and despair than it is to say 'fuck the world' and apply yourself."

"When I was a kid, I'd always be walking up a slide. My Dad used to tell me that if I kept doing that, I'd land on my face. I know what it feels like now, because I've been doing it for years."

Helen lifted my head up and kissed me again.

I felt so safe.

"You need to go to this wedding with your head held high and enjoy yourself, then figure out what you want. Then give it everything you have. No regrets."

"It'll be easier if you come to the wedding with me."

Helen sniggered.

"You're not using me as a crutch, Jason. You've got to face this one alone."

But she was right. There was no hiding place anymore.

"Thank you," I said.

"You're welcome."

There aren't many dates that end in a Game Boy session and a heart-to-heart which surpass a night of steamy lovemaking, but the date with Helen was genuinely the best date I had ever been on. I felt like I had made a genuine connection with her, and I now saw the fact that she was older and a single-parent as a challenge, rather than something to fear or run away from.

I returned home to Sean and Jim feeling good about myself, and they could feel the good vibes radiating from me. It might have been the smell of banana milkshakes, but they looked up from the sofa and smiled anyway.

"Hello, flower," said Jim.

"Good night?" asked Sean.

"Yeah, a really good night," I replied.

"Is Helen your plus one for the wedding?" Jim asked.

"I'm not taking a plus one," I said, triumphantly. "You two are the only plus ones I'll ever need."

I grabbed myself a beer from the kitchen.

Sean and Jim turned to each other, nonplussed.

"That doesn't make any sense," said Jim.

12. Squeaky Bum Time

Three men. One lady. One list of potential gifts with price tags varying from £8 to £495. You couldn't have fitted any more apathy into one shopping centre, but Sean, Jim and I were ready to get Lila a present that showed us how much we cared about her. Then all I needed to know was whether or not Boots sold cyanide pills.

We met at the front of The Shires shopping centre. Amy had brought as much passion and zest for shopping as possible, and was trying to coax it out of us. Sadly, none of us were avid shoppers. Sean bought everything online, Jim had a backpack and no furniture when he moved in and had been wearing the same clothes for the last three years, and my feelings on the subject have already been covered. The question was whether or not we would wear Amy down and bring her to our level of indifference.

"Right. What's the budget?" Amy asked.

"I don't want to buy anything," Jim replied, sparking up a cigarette.

"What's the cheapest thing on there?" Sean asked.

Amy took a deep breath and exhaled. She now understood the position she was in.

"Guys, come on. Help me out a bit?"

I felt a little guilty, and tried to pep things up a little.

"The quicker we get in and get sorted, the quicker we can go and have a beer. There's something I need to tell you anyway," I said.

"You're gay?" said Jim.

I could always count of Jim to be an adult about things.

"No, not that. Not yet. But there's still time so don't give up hope."

Jim laughed and flicked his cigarette into a nearby bin.

"I say we get mathematical about this. We calculate the total cost of the list, divide it by the number of items, and then that will be our budget," I said.

"Deal," Sean agreed.

"Whatever," Jim begrudgingly agreed.

"Cool. Who has a calculator on their phone?" Amy asked.

Jim and I looked at each other, knowing that our phones were one step up from smoke signals. Sean pulled out his Motorola RAZR and started calculating the average cost with Amy's assistance.

"OK, the average is £57," he said.

Jim coughed and frowned at the news.

"Fuck that, she's getting Jamie Oliver tongs and a pint on the night. That's it."

"Jase? What do you think?" Sean asked.

"I say we just buy whatever we want. The more we try and organise this, the more the chavs outside McDonalds are eyeing Sean up for his phone."

Everybody nodded in agreement and headed inside, with Sean keeping a hand on his phone and a watchful eye over his shoulder as he followed.

Deciding what to buy was tough. I didn't want to come across as a skin-flint, but anything too extravagant would be weird, especially as I hadn't seen Lila in over five years. I set myself a budget of £50, and as we looked around the Debenhams home section, Jamie Oliver was staring at us with those cheeky chappy eyes of his, enticing us to buy his bowls and kitchen gadgets.

Jim turned his nose up yet again as he gazed over the kitchenware.

"I've never read a wedding list with more kitchenware on it. Bread makers, bowls and bollocks. Is she planning on being a housewife or is he one of those knobs who puts dinner parties on for his pretentious twatty mates?"

"He's going to be so happy to meet you," Amy said.

"Have you actually met him?" I asked, seizing my opportunity to feel better about myself by finding out the groom was a bellend.

"Yeah, he's lovely. He's a web designer."

"What the fuck does that mean?" Jim asked.

"He designs websites for businesses. He's pretty minted, or so I hear."

That backfired.

I grabbed a £16 mortar and pestle and turned to Amy, who looked surprised that I was the first to fold and purchase any old crap from the list.

"No romantic send-off? No metaphorical gift with a hidden message?" she asked.

"Nope. Just a tool for grinding the fuck out of some spices."

Amy could see that I couldn't hide it any longer. The wedding was getting closer, and the thought of putting effort into finding a gift with some kind of hidden meaning didn't sit well with me anymore. I just wanted it to be over so I could book my Australia tickets and get out of everyone's lives for a while.

After much faffing about, Amy, Sean and Jim made their decisions and we met at the tills to pay up. As we stood in the queue, each holding our gifts, Sean and Jim looked down at my small mortar and pestle, then back to each other, before shrugging their shoulders. They had opted for a bread maker and a 16 piece dining set respectively, much bigger gifts than I had gone for, and they were confused by my choice of such a small and inconsequential gift.

"My mate Trev used to use one of them to make his weed mix," said Sean.

"I'll be sure to recommend that to them when I see them," I snapped.

Sean decided that trying to make conversation was a bad idea, and we paid for our gifts and left the store in silence.

When we stepped outside, Amy gave us all a kiss and a hug as she prepared to leave us for the afternoon.

"Looks like my work here is done," she said. "You guys can relax now."

"Sorry I was a dick earlier. I hate shopping. Drives me nuts," said Jim, looking like a sad dog that had been left out in the rain all day.

"That's OK, Jim. I'll see you at the wedding, yeah? We'll grab a table for the old college legends."

"Sounds good," I said.

Amy waved to us as she left, and Sean's eyes followed her down the street.

"I wish I'd made a move on her when we were at college," he said.

"You guys kill me," Jim laughed. "Your cocks are there to be used. You know that, right?"

We headed off to the pub, looking like three old ladies on a shopping trip.

The White House was dead in the afternoons, and this made it easier for me to keep Jim and Sean from being distracted by Sky Sports and uni girls. I bought a round of beers, and prepared myself for dishing out the bad news.

"Right guys, I've got something to tell you… I'm leaving."

"Thank fuck!" said Jim.

"That's great news!" said Sean.

Not the reaction I was expecting. Deflated, I took a sip of my pint to collect myself.

"I thought you'd be disappointed?"

"What's there to be disappointed about? You've left your shit job, you somehow managed to empty your nuts with the aid of a woman, and you're going to Australia. What could be bad about that?"

Jim's enthusiasm was nice to hear, but I was confused as to how he knew all of this information.

"How did you know about Australia?" I asked.

"This guy at work had told me about this porn film that was insane, and you've got the biggest computer screen, so I logged on and found all of your Aussie stuff in your search history."

"Thanks for your honesty." I said.

"You're welcome," he replied.

"Great news, buddy," Sean chimed in. "We couldn't be happier for you. It'll be a great experience for you and you'll come back refreshed and eager for the next step. Couldn't be more chuffed for you."

Despite the fact that Jim had hacked into my password-protected computer in the hope of finding porn and uncovered my plans, both his and Sean's enthusiasm was much appreciated. It made me feel like I was making the right decision, despite the fact that I made it in the time it takes Justin Gatlin to run the 100 metres.

"Aren't you pissed off with me for not discussing it with you though?" I asked.

"Of course not, we've wanted you out for ages." Jim joked.

"We'll find a way to carry on without you moping around and talking about muscly black men fighting each other." Sean joined in.

I couldn't have been happier at how easily the 'I'm moving out' conversation had gone. In all honesty, we were all going to benefit from the break-up. As a band, we were in *Be Here Now* territory, where the tunes were still there but they lacked the freshness of the previous albums. We needed to disband triumphantly before heading into *Standing on the Shoulder of Giants* territory.

No friendship deserves that.

The wedding was only a few short days away, and I spent most of them packing up my things and changing the lease so that Jim and Sean would be the names on the house. The rental agency were a little pissed that I hadn't actually told them that anyone else had been living there, but the lease passed over without too much trouble. The guys gave me my deposit back early as a going away present too, which was really good of them. At least I'd have some money to spend in Australia now, and could put off fighting off redbacks in the fields for a few weeks.

Dad hired a white van to move me out of the house, and spent most of the morning laughing at how little stuff I had accumulated over the past few years. With the exception of my DVD and VHS cabinets, a Hi-Fi, TV, DVD player and a coffee table, I told the guys that they could keep everything else. 'Everything else' was a dodgy microwave and some pots and pans, which explained why they didn't thank me and Jim gave me the 'wanker' sign.

I moved my belongings into the spare bedroom, before taking a minute to soak up my situation. I had just moved out of my own place and back into my folks' house, where I hadn't lived for five years. It was starting to dawn on me that I was going to see my dream girl for the first time in years, and she was going to think I was a fucking loser.

I lay on my new/old bed and texted Helen, in the hope that she would make me feel better about myself.

"HELLO. HOW ARE YOU AND BUDDY MOLLY? EVERYTHING GOOD?"

The reply came back straight away.

"V.GOOD. TALKING ABOUT YOU LAST NIGHT WITH MOLZ. SHE'S STUCK ON THE GHOST SHIP."

I used to hate that fucking level. I felt a duty to reply and encourage.

"TELL HER NOT TO PANIC WHEN SHE'S SWIMMING TOWARDS THE GHOSTS. BE CALM AND SWIM CAREFULLY. SHE'LL BE FINE."

"I'M SO HAPPY THAT I CAN BE THE MARIO MESSENGER FOR YOU TWO."

"AWW, YOU'RE SO MUCH MORE THAN THAT. YOU'RE THE CHIEF MILKSHAKE MAKER."

I caught myself smiling like a fool as I text back. Even through SMS, Helen and I seemed to have a rapport. But now I was going to head off to Oz and kill it before it had even begun. I needed to tell her as soon as the wedding was over. In the meantime, a little flirt was in order.

"I KEEP THINKING ABOUT YOU IN THAT BLACK DRESS YOU WORE ON OUR FIRST DATE. YOU LOOKED AMAZING."

"I KNOW. I WAS THERE."

I laughed and texted back.

"WHY DO YOU ALWAYS DEFLECT A COMPLIMENT WITH HUMOUR?"

No reply. Time stands still when you're waiting for a text message.

Then it came through, albeit one that I didn't want.

"MOLLY'S DAD IS HERE. DON'T WANT TO BE RUDE. I'LL TEXT YOU LATER. ENJOY THE WEDDING. ARRRRRRRRGH!!! DON'T GET DRUNK AND TELL HER YOU LOVE HER. BAD FORM. XXX"

I put the phone down and sighed.

The morning of the wedding was horrendous. The clothes I planned to wear seemed cheap and nasty, my hair was a mess and needed cutting, and I was angry at myself for being an arse and buying a caveman tool for a wedding gift. When mum saw the gift, she shook her head and slipped £50 into a card. "You can do better than that," she said. I don't think she was talking about the gift.

The good news was that mum had cooked the biggest breakfast ever for the arrival of Sean and Jim, who were coming over to spend the morning with me before heading back to Leicester for the evening reception. Jim had text me at 6am to make sure I hadn't killed myself, which was nice of him.

My nostrils were instantly hit with the smell of bacon. I changed to a veggie for a year once because I'd never smoked and wanted to see if I had any willpower. The experiment was only ever difficult when bacon was around.

Quorn couldn't fake bacon for shit.

Mum smiled at me as she set the table for her guest's arrival.

"So the rumours are true," she said. "Duran Duran have reformed."

"We have. So be nice or I'll sing 'Wild Boys'," I said, trying to flatten my bed head.

I sat down at the table and waited for Sean and Jim's imminent arrival.

"What time do you have to be there tonight?" Mum asked.

"7pm."

"Do you know what time the wedding is?"

"Noon, as far as I know."

I hadn't even considered the ceremony itself. At 12pm, I would be sitting on my parents' sofa thinking about what I'm going to say to Lila. She would be saying her vowels and reducing her family to tears of joy.

The sound of the letterbox opening threw me out of my daydream and I collected the post. Anything to keep my mind off the bacon. Amongst the pile of bills and Farmfoods leaflets was a letter addressed to mum's business. I took this as an opportunity to talk to her about it, in the hope that she would open up more.

"You've got a business letter here," I said, holding it out to her.

Mum backed away as if the letter was on fire, but I kept my arm outstretched so that she had to take it from me.

"You can't hide from it. It meant the world to you," I said.

"'Meant' being the operative word. Throw it away. It will just be some marketing thing anyway."

"You won't know until you open it."

The letter was almost under her nose by this point. Mum grabbed it from my hand and threw it in the kitchen bin. Now I felt awful.

"I'm sorry. I just don't want you to stop caring."

"I cared too much. That was the problem."

"But you tried to do everything alone. You should have talked to Dad."

Mum laughed, sadly.

"Your dad doesn't help with anything besides paying the bills and walking the dog. You know what he's like."

"Try him. You'll be surprised."

Mum smiled at me, and I felt the sudden urge to apologise to her. After all, I had been just as self-involved and absent as dad.

"I wish I could have been more involved."

"You've got your own life to lead. Now go and eat your breakfast. Sean and Jim can play catch up since neither of them own a watch."

I gave Mum a huge squeeze and a kiss on the top of her head. She rubbed my back and smacked me on the bum in her usual 'Now go!' way. I took the hint and headed to the breakfast table.

I hadn't been feasting long when Jim and Sean came crashing through the door, hugging and swinging mum around. She loved it.

"Hello boys, do you want some breakfast?" she said.

"Is the Pope Jewish?" Jim said, excitedly.

Sean rolled his eyes at Jim's stupidity.

They joined me at the table and munched away on bacon, sausages, hash browns, beans, fried bread, mushrooms and more. It was a beast of a feast, and when it was done, Jim offered to do the washing up, which came as a surprise to Sean and me, as the lazy bastard had never lifted a finger to do it at our place. It was clearly a tactic to soften mum up, and it had worked.

After Jim's attempts at housekeeping had finished, we sat at the table and talked about the wedding, and my plans to take Australia by storm. Mum was pretty blasé about the backpacking trip, as if she wasn't entirely convinced I would end up going. She was more interested in what Jim was up to. It was more exciting, to be fair.

"How's the army then, Jim?" she asked.

"Good," he said.

Jim paused for a moment, before hitting us with a bombshell.

"I'm going to Iraq."

Sean nodded and smiled like a proud dog owner at Crufts. He had already been informed.

I felt sick to my stomach.

"Are you nervous?" Mum asked.

"Not at all, I can't wait. But if I watched Sky News all day, I'd probably fill my pants."

"A friend from my… from work told me that her son went and it was unbearably hot. He said that the majority of locals were very nice though."

"I'm sure I'll be sunbathing for six months," Jim said, giving mum a reassuring smile.

"Try and go to Dubai while you're out there. I met Gazza at the Wild Wadi water park," Sean said.

That was enough for me. I had to say my piece.

"I can't believe how nonchalant you're all being about something so serious! How long have you known about this?" I said.

"Eight months," Jim said.

Shocked, I looked at Sean and waited for his answer.

"Last week," he said.

"I'm a bit pissed off at both of you, if I'm honest. You should've told me. This is a big deal."

Jim rolled his eyes at me and laughed.

"You were always going to be the last person I told about this. No offence, but did you really expect me to tell you after the way you responded to Lila's wedding? You make Woody Allen sound like John McClane, you big fanny."

Jim panicked and apologised to mum for using the word 'fanny', but she was too busy agreeing with him to take offence.

"Not everyone in the Middle East is a suicide-bombing lapdog of Al Qaeda, buddy," Jim said.

"I know that. I just feel guilty about how much I've been banging on about me and my problems."

"Watching you implode kept my mind off it, so don't feel bad."

Mum and Sean sniggered. After a few moments, I allowed myself to join in.

When it came to 12 o'clock, I took myself away from everyone and spent five minutes in the conservatory, looking out over the garden that dad had spent so much time working on. I thought about Lila, and played out the entire wedding ceremony in my head. My stomach turned as the church bells rang, but at the same time, I felt an overwhelming sense of joy for Lila and her website-making husband. They had found in their early twenties what can elude people their entire lives. I hoped that I wouldn't be one of them.

Jim wandered in and sat next to me. He didn't say anything, just gave me a comforting smile and looked out over the garden with me. It wasn't long until Sean followed and did the same.

"Are you wearing your uniform tonight?" I asked.

"Of course. In the current climate, war is sexy."

Sean laughed and shook his head.

"This is going to be the last time we do anything like this for ages," he said. "Let's make the most of it, yeah?"

Jim leapt forward and squeezed myself and Sean has hard as he could.

"I love you guys, I really do. I'll be thinking of you every day when I'm disposing IEDs."

"Please don't think of us when you need to concentrate on not blowing up," said Sean.

A couple of hours later, I was trying my suit on when mum knocked on the door. Fortunately it still fitted, and the dry cleaning meant that the suit didn't smell like breakfast anymore. Yes, I was going to be wearing the infamous suit I wore for work, you judgemental bastards.

I spread my arms out so mum could get a good look at me.

"How do I look?" I asked.

"Perfect!"

"I thought so."

Mum rolled her eyes at me. She started fiddling with my tie, which is something that all women do, not just mums. It must have a honing beacon attached to it. Either that or all men are shit with ties?

"This girl meant a lot to you. I think what you're doing is very brave, and mature."

Mum left me to my own devices, which for me was imitating an ageing Jake LaMotta in the mirror, throwing punches and grunting "I'm the boss, I'm the boss, I'm the boss…" before brushing myself down and heading downstairs to meet Sean and Jim.

They were waiting for me at the door, having said goodbye to mum and stealing another kiss and a cuddle from her.

"Are you ready to rock?" asked Sean.

"I have no idea."

13. Nice Day for a Shite Wedding

There is nothing more surreal than walking towards your ex-workplace just a few weeks after they sacked you, dressed in the suit you were wearing when you were fired, no less. Oh, and it's going to be the first time you've seen the love of your life in five years, and she's the fucking bride.

The closer I got to the entrance of the hotel, the more I wanted to do a Sir Robin, and gallantly chicken out and run away. Fortunately I had Sean and Jim either side of me as support, even if they did have bets as to whether or not I would be kicked off the premises within five minutes.

Jim had drawn the short straw and was carrying the wedding gifts, although it would've made more sense for me to have them so I could hide my face in the event of an emergency.

We looked around for signs of life as we stepped into the hotel. Both the reception and lobby area were quiet, just a few guests checking in here and there. To the left of the doors was the conference and banqueting area, where the wedding guests were mingling.

Jim pinned his shoulders back and lead us towards them.

"Come on you pussies, let's get a drink."

I pulled Jim back for a quick pep talk.

"Look. I just wanted to say before we go any further, that I love you both. Thank you, for everything. Not just today, but always."

"You're welcome, buddy." Sean said.

Jim looked up at the lights and then back to us. He had his annoyed-child face on again.

"Can I get drunk and have sex with a complete stranger now, please? I've got my Iraq story to use and no time to lose."

"Sorry. Are you sure the Iraq story won't just make them cry?" I said.

"It made Sean cry."

"What? I don't cry," Sean said, in a poor attempt at being macho.

"If I flick your balls, you will retract that statement."

I decided that it was best to put the soppiness to one side and concentrate on getting settled, and that meant getting a drink. Fortunately, Craig was standing at a welcome drinks table. He handed us a glass of champagne each as we approached.

"Three glasses of piss," he said.

"Cheers, Craig. These are my two friends, Jim and Sean."

"How's it going?" asked Craig, shaking their hands.

"Good, good. He's not going to get kicked out is he?" asked Sean.

"No. He can stay if he takes this tray to the kitchen for me," he laughed, still a bastard. "Don't worry, you're free to get smashed, and Mike's not in charge of the food either."

In a moment of weakness, I allowed my soppy side to rear its ugly head again.

"I just wanted to say thank you, for everything."

Craig turned to Sean and Jim in horror.

"He keeps doing that to us, too," said Jim.

"Get drunk or get fucked," said Craig, shooing us away from the table like you would a stray cat.

"I plan on doing both, friend," Jim replied.

Craig raised a glass to us, and we walked through to the main area. Sean huddled in for a status check.

"Are we OK, then? You're not going to get kicked out?"

"Nah, Craig's cool. Just don't put your card behind the bar unless you want it to be raped."

"Fuck that, when the cash runs out I'm nicking the wine off the tables."

"You classy bastard."

Sean pointed out Amy and her fiancé Dave in a crowd of strangers. I scanned the rest of the crowd, looking for a hint of white that would lead me to Lila. She was nowhere to be seen. No doubt she was being swamped with attention from the family and friends who had actually seen her in the past half a decade.

Amy and Dave came over and we all clinked our champagne flutes together.

"Legends! How are you?" asked Amy.

"Good, thanks. You look awesome," I said.

"Cheers. You remember Dave don't you?"

"I do indeed. How are you, buddy?"

"I'm good thanks," said Dave. "Are you nervous?"

"No…" I replied, blatantly lying.

"Wait until you see her," he said.

"How are you feeling?" Amy asked.

"He's turned gay," Sean butted in.

"Ha-ha! I've made peace with everything. I'm here to have a good time," I said.

"Denial!" Jim shouted from behind me, before barging through and shaking Dave's hand.

"Right you fuckers, I'm off to get rid of these wanky presents and tell a girl it's my last day before Iraq. I'll catch up with you later."

Jim headed off into the crowd. Dave turned to me and shook his head.

"Bloody hell, he hasn't changed."

"And he never will. At least until someone fires a rocket launcher at his head," I said.

Dave put his hand on my arm and looked puzzled.

"Is he seriously going to Iraq? I thought he'd come in fancy dress."

Amy put her hands to her face and sighed.

Sean and I necked our champagne and headed to the bar to get a drink that didn't taste like piss and give us acid reflux. We left Amy to explain to her soon-to-be-husband that Jim wasn't the only person in the history of formal weddings to come in fancy dress, but was in fact a member of the Armed Forces.

Karen, a uni student who worked on the bar part-time, met us with a smile. She leaned over the bar and kissed me on the cheek.

"That wasn't very professional, but fuck it, we've missed you," she said.

"Bless you, I miss the people, but not the place."

"I hear you. What can I get you? Oh, and by the way, the fat obnoxious fucker at the end of the bar has a tab open and he's pissed already."

Words like those were music to Sean's ears. He barged in front me and ordered for us.

"Two double JD and Coke's and two Sambucas, please."

"Coming right up."

I gave Sean my "What the fuck?" face. He smirked at me, knowing that we needed to get on it if I was ever going to relax and enjoy the evening.

Karen put the drinks on the bar and continued serving the other guests. Sean checked her out before turning to me.

"And you *didn't* want to work here anymore?"

Sean handed me the Sambuca first, which is always a good idea for a first drink at a wedding reception.

"Here's to swimming with bowlegged women," Sean said, before dropping his shot of Sambuca down the hatch and giving me intense feelings of déjà vu.

Sean ignored me and pushed a shot glass under my nose. I took it from him and guzzled it down, before pulling a face like someone had just smeared Dave's Insanity Sauce on my top lip. Why does anyone drink that aniseed abomination? No good can ever come of it.

Sean pointed to Jim, who was at the end of the bar talking to a pretty girl in her early twenties. We shuffled down the bar so we could hear what he was saying to her.

"Three of my best friends have died and it's time for some motherfucking revenge…"

Sean and I burst out laughing. It sounded like the trailer for a Dolph Lundgren film, but the girl was lapping it up, so the joke was on us. And as my recent track record consisted of one drunk girl whose bearded friend was breathing into my ear the majority of the time, I wasn't really in a position to judge.

Sean looked around at the wedding guests surrounding the bar. The vast majority of them were old, which prompted Sean to order more shots.

"Are you trying to kill me?" I asked.

"Look around you. Half the guests smell like piss and biscuits. I'm surprised they're not serving Earl Grey instead of fucking Champers. We are going to drink some shots, dance like twats and you are going to meet Lila with a full bag of beans. OK?"

Sean could be pretty forceful when he had an idea in his head, and a bar covered in shot glasses.

We nailed a couple more shots before entering the reception room. It was decked out nicely, and Sean and I wandered over to the gift table. There were dozens of envelopes in a small basket, and our gifts were placed with the others. I looked at my tiny box and instantly regretted not getting a better gift.

"I am such a whopper," I said.

Sean was too busy checking out the female guests to hear or answer me.

"This is better," he said. "They must have told the old people to stay out of the room."

I looked at my watch. It had just passed 7:45, which meant that the cutting of the cake and first dance would be coming up soon. I searched the room for signs of Lila, but still she eluded me.

Sean and I went back to the bar to take advantage of the free-for-all. Two more double JDs were skulled, along with a couple of Sambucas. I could feel myself starting to wane already, and we'd only been at the hotel for an hour. The pressure was making me nervous, and my nerves were making me drink. At this rate, by the time I spoke to Lila I would open my mouth to speak and cover her in a cocktail of bile and aniseed.

Jim was now talking to three girls about his upcoming trip to Iraq, and they were engrossed. I overheard him talking about the 'punishing training regime' he had been undertaking for the last eight weeks in preparation for his mission. I felt like butting in and telling the girls that Jim's training regime consisted of smoking cigarettes and masturbating. I chose to let him have his fun instead.

A familiar face came over to say hello. It took us a while to put a name to the face, but we soon discovered that it was Tom, our old college friend. It brought back memories of the socials we used to attend, and it looked like those nights spent at the bar with Sean and I had become a precedent for the years that followed, which explained why his face was redder than a baboons backside and he couldn't say more than five words without taking a drink, burping or farting, both of which smelt like death.

"Have you seen the bride yet?" Tom asked.

"No. You?"

"Just chatted with her. Fiiiiiiiiiiiit," he said.

"Yeah?"

"Oh yeah, unbelievable. You used to shag her didn't you? I remember someone shagging her?"

For some reason, Tom's voice went up in volume when he used the word 'shag', which prompted wedding guests to turn around and look at us. Sean didn't care, but I did. If somebody told Lila that we were mouthing off, our first meeting in years would be a nightmare, not to mention our last.

"No. I dated her a couple of times," I said, before prompting a fast subject change. "What have you been up to?"

"Telebanking and a lot of drinking. I live next door to a pub in Preston."

No shit.

"Ah, nice one," I said.

"What about you?"

Sean decided that this would be the perfect opportunity for me to accept what had happened to me and move on.

"He got sacked from this place a few weeks ago for dropping eggs down himself and telling an entire restaurant filled with customers to go fuck themselves."

Thanks, Sean.

Tom didn't even bat an eyelid.

"Excellent. Excellent."

Tom tottered off to find someone else to talk to, and I gave Sean a dead arm.

"What the fuck was that?" I said.

"Look, man. You're having a good time, and you're fucking off to the other side of the world. Who cares what people think of you? They'll never see you again."

He had a point, even if he demonstrated it in spectacularly shitbag fashion.

"How are you feeling?" he asked.

"I'm pretty drunk. I should probably cool it for a while. At least until after the cake, dance and all the formalities."

"Good idea. One more shot, and then a rest."

It wasn't quite what I meant, but the drinks were going down nicely and having the desired effect. I was loosening up and feeling less self-conscious, which was a huge bonus.

George, the Conference and Banqueting Manager, came over and stood at the bar. He looked over the guests and cleared his throat.

"Ladies and gentlemen, please make your way into the main room for the cutting of the cake, followed by the bride and groom's first dance as a married couple."

The hordes of old ancestors and family friends made their way into the main room, followed by the third level of guests – namely myself, Sean, Jim and other school friends – and some other stragglers.

Somehow I found myself standing behind Lurch from *The Addams Family* and The Tooth Fairy from *Manhunter*, which meant I couldn't see a damn thing. Sean and Jim had managed to sneak their way in front of me, but I was too polite to ask people to move or barge my way through.

Cameras started to flash, and the guests cheered and cooed at the cutting of the cake, which I couldn't see. I could make out the cartoony bride and groom cake decorations on the top tier, and the top of Lila and her husband's heads, but that was all. I joined in the applause, but I still hadn't seen Lila.

An opportunity to pass between the two giants came up, and I stood next to Jim and Sean, where I got my first glimpse of Lila Holmes in five years.

She looked heartbreakingly beautiful, her make-up simple, which brought out those huge brown eyes that you could swim in, her dress divine and showing off that perfect body. One of her cutest traits – one that she must have been doing all day and was doing in this moment – was that she would put her hand up to her mouth when she laughed enough to show her teeth.

Seeing Lila looking so beautiful and content – mixed with being a little too tipsy for 8pm on a Friday – made me reach for the bottle of red wine that was staring seductively from the table next to me.

Sean turned to me and tried to take the bottle of wine from my hand, but I shook my head in defiance and started drinking from it. It suddenly dawned on Sean that feeding me Sambuca might not have been a good idea after all, and that there was a good chance that it would be downhill from here.

The lights dimmed, and the crowd fell silent.

"What's that?" I asked.

Sean sighed.

"The prolonging of your misery."

A familiar song started to play, and Lila and Mark came together and started to dance to it. The song wouldn't have been familiar to many people in the audience, but I knew it well, because I had introduced Lila to both the song and the artist.

It was the last straw for me. The red wine was gone by the time Jeff Buckley even reached the chorus of 'Everybody Here Wants You', and as I watched Lila and Mark dancing and gazing into each other's eyes, I thought back to the moment when I introduced Lila to the song…

Lila was laying on my bed, reading the sleeve notes for *Sketches for My Sweetheart the Drunk*. I was listening and wishing that he hadn't gone swimming that night on May 29, 1997.

"He's dead?" Lila said, shocked.

"Yep. Thirty years old, what a waste," I said.

I jumped onto the bed and we lay with each other as Jeff told his story.

Back in the real world, Lila and Mark were still dancing, and I continued to torture myself. I reached for another bottle of wine, but as I did, I almost knocked it off the table. I quickly regained my balance and decided that now was a good time to have a moment to myself.

I made my way through the wedding guests, bowing my head so not to make eye contact with anyone. Sean watched me leave, and was torn between being a good friend and a good wedding guest. One person leaving during the first dance could be written off as bladder control problems. Two people is a situation. Sean opted to wait for the end of the song. Jim was oblivious to everything, watching the married couple dance like a proud grandmother.

I made my way to the men's toilets, and threw water on my face to sober up and drag myself out of this depressive daydream. I could still hear the song through the walls, and it was coming to an end. This wasn't much comfort to me, as I used to quote one of the songs final lines to Lila whenever she would get mardy with me, or if I wanted to try and come across as a hopeless romantic, rather than just hopeless.

Hearing the end of the song brought back memories of all the times when I had tried – with mixed results – to make Lila understand what I didn't even understand myself at the time: That I loved her and would've done anything for her. But I didn't, so what the fuck was I doing at her wedding?

A huge man who barely fitted into his evening suit walked in and squeezed himself into a cubicle. He sat down, let out a squeaker, and then unloaded his entire wedding breakfast into the pan. Cheers buddy. Nothing kills a moment of nostalgia better than a fat man using the shithouse.

Sean came in looking for me. If he'd turned around he would've seen me right away, but instead, he went straight to the cubicle of the fat guy and knocked on the door four times.

"Come on. You know that four knocks is the secret code for 'naughty time."

Sean stood back and chuckled to himself. Even in my depressive state, I couldn't pass up the opportunity to witness what was coming.

The toilet flushed, and the fat man bundled his way out of the cubicle. He frowned at an open-mouthed and embarrassed Sean.

"Wanker," he said.

The fat man washed his hands and left the men's room as fast as his chubby middle-aged legs could carry him. Sean turned to see me giggling like a four-year-old at the wash basins.

"Could've told me he was there," he said.

"It was too good to pass up."

"Yeah. I'd have done the same, to be fair."

"This is too important for you to fuck up now. You haven't even seen Lila yet."

"I know. It was the song."

"Everything you see and hear tonight is going to remind you of that stuff. You knew this on day one."

"I thought I was better prepared than this."

"It's partly my fault. Fucking Sambuca."

"It's not your fault, or Sambuca's. It's mine, and mine alone. I'm a fucking child."

"No you're not, you're a man. You've just got to re-attach your balls and go and speak to Lila. Once you do that, everything will be fine. Stop building everything up in your mind and roll with it. Otherwise you're going to get kicked out for being drunk and you'll never move on. This is your only chance, and you have to make a choice. Are you Jason Chapman, my friend, the smart guy who everyone likes and has time for, or are you the guy who turns up at the wedding, gets drunk, treads on the kids, cries a lot, turns racist after 12 pints and sings 'Angels' at full volume whilst sweating all over the bride and groom?"

I took a moment to let all of those graphic details sink in.

"Was that a generalisation?" I asked.

"My dad. Every fucking wedding…"

"Right."

Sean nudged me again, and we shared a smile. Then he bear-hugged me and kissed me on the top of my head.

"Did you throw up?" he asked.

"Yup."

"How was it?"

"Helpful."

"Delightful. Have a mint."

Sean handed me a box of Tic-Tacs. I devoured half the box before handing it back to Sean.

"Better?" he asked.

"Definitely. I love the smell of Tic-Tacs. They smell like childhood."

"OK. I think you've lived in the past for long enough. Let's get you back into the present."

Sean took me by the arms and shook me.

"I didn't want to say anything bad about Lila, it being her wedding and you being a little bit one-sided in your memories of her, but she was – and probably still is – a massive pain in the arse. She turned you into a fucking wreck of a human being, and she liked doing it, too. She was an attention-seeking little bitch, and all of your friends hated what she did to you. Can't you remember how much of a cock tease she was? How much she used to wind you up and try and make you jealous?"

I bowed my head in shame. He was right. Every word was true.

"She's a sweet girl, but she's not the right girl for you. Never was. And that means the right one is still out there. You might've already met her. Look, man, this doesn't have to be painful. Enjoy it for fucks sake. You'll be in Oz soon, and you'll have snakes and spiders to worry about. Women will be the least of your worries."

Sean's mixture of kind words, reality checks and drunken ramblings about his dad had won me round, and we put our arms around each other as we left the toilets with stupid grins on our faces.

"We're walking out of the men's toilets with your arms around each other, having entered separately," I pointed out.

"Let 'em talk. I don't care."

The guests had spilled out into the main lobby following the first dance, and we noticed that Jim was standing with Mark, Lila's husband. This was my chance to take some of the pain away from the evening.

Mark smiled as Sean and I approached, and all I could think was *"Please be a dick, please be a dick, please be a dick, please be a dick."*

He held out his hand for us to shake, and we both obliged.

"Where have you two ball bags been? This is Mark, Lila's hubby. He's one cool hombre," said Jim.

As much as it killed me to accept it at the time, Mark seemed like a genuine, down-to-earth guy. It was difficult for me not to hate him on principal alone, but he had an innate likeability about him. I could see why Lila would fall for someone like him.

"Nice to meet you, and congrats," I said.

I would like to thank BAFTA for recognising my acting talents.

"Thank you," Mark replied.

"We apologise for Jim. He's getting killed in a few days," said Sean.

Mark burst into laughter.

"Lila said you guys were funny. She talks about you all the time. Sounds like you guys had a great time together at college."

"Oh, it wasn't too bad," I said.

"It was too bad, which is why we're uneducated and only partially sober," said Sean.

"Ah well, at least you're enjoying yourselves."

"Definitely," we said.

"Now if you'll excuse me, I've got to do the rounds. If I stand still for more than two seconds I get attacked. I'll catch up with you later when the oldies fuck off to bed and the dancefloor beckons, yeah?"

Mark vanished before any of us could even answer him. There were approximately one hundred and fifty people in and around the room, and they were there just to see him and his wife.

I glanced over at Jim, who was looking a little melancholy.

"Are you OK, buddy?" I asked.

"Yeah. It's just sinking in that we're growing up, y'know?"

"Fucking hell. What's wrong with you two?" Sean said.

"Don't you feel the winds of change?" Jim said.

"I thought that was just Tom's beer farts, but maybe. I dunno..."

I put my arm around Jim and gave him a friendly shake.

"It's a new beginning, buddy. The next time we see each other you'll be a war hero, I'll have a tan, and Sean will be wearing leather pants and have a boyfriend called Nigel."

Sean and Jim laughed, and we raised our glasses. Before I could make a toast to something clichéd like 'the next step' or 'the future', a familiar voice came from behind me.

"What are we toasting?"

I spun around, and found myself face-to-face with Lila Holmes for the first time in five years.

Sink or swim.

I swallowed, smiled, and stood up straight.

"You," I said.

14. The Reunion

Lila dragged me away from Sean, Jim and – more importantly – her husband and wedding guests, and around to the main restaurant and bar area.

We sat in the darkest corner of the bar and let the approaching waitress know that we didn't need anything but a chance to talk.

I sat opposite Lila and examined her closely for any faults. She was perfection, as always. It took me a while before I could speak to her without sounding like a shy teenage boy with a crush.

"Alone at last," said Lila, as she tried to entangle her long dress from around her feet so that she wouldn't face plant onto the table when she stood up again.

"I know. You look incredible. You soar."

Lila smiled, then gave me a look that said "Explain?"

"Soar. Some girls merely walk through life. The better ones glide. But the crème de la crème… they soar."

Lila let that sink in for a moment.

"I like it. I've never heard it before."

"I always aim high… If I'm honest though, I kinda stole it from Andy Garcia."

"If you're going to plagiarise, it might as well be Andy Garcia, the greatest philosopher that ever lived."

"Personally, I'm a big fan of his work."

Lila laughed, and did the thing where she put her hand to her mouth to hide her teeth again. I had to be careful not to fall in love with her again, which would be difficult if she kept doing that.

"Let's get serious for a moment. What have I missed in the last few years? Update me."

"I'm married with three kids. One of each."

Hand to the mouth again.

Stop making her laugh you dick. You're just going to make it worse.

"Be serious, clown! The suit is nice and you smell expensive. What have you been doing to earn your dough?"

"I'm unemployed. I just made one last effort for you."

"Ah, thank you. I don't believe you, but thank you."

"Believe me. I have no idea what I'm doing, where I'm going. The past few weeks have been the worst of my life. And it all started with your invite."

Lila's eyes widened at the last comment. Before that, she was probably more concerned that she might have a suicide at her wedding reception. But now, there was something else to consider: the fact that she still had a hold on me.

"I wish I could say that I felt bad for you," she said.

"What do you mean?" I asked, both offended and deflated.

"It's good to hear that I can still make an impact in your life," she said, smiling and waiting for a witty response.

"Effortless," I said.

One of my all-time favourite film scenes is the 'uncomfortable silence' scene from *Pulp Fiction*. At Jack Rabbit Slims, Vincent Vega and Mia Wallace sit opposite each other and share a comfortable silence, and the audience shares it too. Mia tells Vincent it's a sign that you've found someone special.

Lila and I used to sit for hours in each other's company and hardly say a word, and I would always be reminded of that scene. I couldn't believe that we still had it, even now, as she sat across from me in her wedding dress.

Lila knew it too, and she made the wise decision to break our comfortable silence before a wedding guest found us and broke it before we'd had a chance to catch up properly.

"Five – friggin' – years!" she said.

"I know. Where did the years go…? *Why* did the years go?"

"Tell me about it."

"Ah, shuddup! You still look a-maz-ing. I look like a fat Ben Affleck."

"Silly! So you haven't brought a girlfriend?"

"Just Sean and Jim."

"Those guys!"

"Yeah, no girlfriend. You gave me dream girl syndrome."

"Forgive me!"

"I do. I can't hold a candle for you forever, I don't have the upper body strength."

Lila took a close look at me, for signs that I was joking. She looked down at the table and shook her head.

"I'm no dream girl. That was always your problem."

I picked up on the change of mood.

"What do you mean?"

"You always expected so much from me. You put me on this pedestal and kept building me up. I could never live up to it. It smothered me."

"I'm sorry. I didn't mean to."

"I would go home every day after being told by you I was 'perfect' and 'the one', and my step-father would be telling me the exact opposite. I didn't know who to believe."

"I was right. He was an asshole."

"No. That's just the thing. You were both wrong. I wasn't useless, or a horrible piece of crap, but I wasn't the perfect girl either. It took me a lot of time to figure it out, and that's when I met Mark, and he took me at face value. Always has."

This time, the comfortable silence wasn't comfortable at all. But it was deafening. If I had just stepped back and asked Lila about what she was feeling back then, instead of pouring affection on her, maybe things would have been different.

Now seemed like as good a time as any to forget the past and concentrate on the present and the future.

"Mark seems like a great guy. For what it's worth, I'm happy for you. I'd watch out though, Jim's smitten with him."

"Should I be worried?"

"Terrified. The guy has eight years' experience of watching *Platoon*."

Lila laughed. She took my hands in hers and squeezed them.

"There were times with you that I just wanted to smash your head in, just to make you see sense. You infuriated me."

"I'm not a doctor, but I'm pretty sure that smashing my head in wouldn't make me see sense…"

Lila butted in.

"Stop joking. You know what I mean."

It was my turn to stare down at the table and do the confessional thing.

"I know I was needy, and more than a little pathetic, but you were impossible to read back then. I didn't know enough about what was going on to help you, and even if I did, I would have just played Jeff Buckley to you… Oh, and by the way, thanks for killing me with that song."

"The first dance? There was never another choice. I guess I should thank you."

"Yep."

"Thank you."

"You're welcome."

Lila exhaled and threw my hands away.

"Right. Now we've sorted our issues out, let's get to the bottom of this 'no girlfriend' thing. Don't be a pussy and blame me. What's wrong with you? You're funny, nice smile, eyes, great arse!"

"Yeah, I've still got that! It's weird, no matter how fat I get the arse stays round and pert. It floats. Line up the bridesmaids!"

"No! No, no, no, no. Damaged goods. Christ, listen to me. I'm such a bitch! I'm still protective of you. You deserve the 'soarers'. Is that even a word?

"Who cares? You're paying me compliments. Most girls just pour rice all over me."

Lila recoiled in her chair.

"Oh, Steph..." she said.

Will there ever be an end to my misery?

"What do you know about that?"

"Don't worry. You shared some food. She went to make you a coffee and you fell asleep with the plate on you and it tipped over."

"Ever the romantic."

"You can sleep again now."

"I've been trying to work out how that happened for weeks now. How the hell did you hear about it?"

"Facebook."

"Whatty-what-now?"

"Facebook. It's taking over from MySpace as the new internetty, socially-networky thingy. You set up an account and old friends can get in touch with you, pretend they still care about you and then perv over your holiday pictures."

"Sounds amazing."

"Revolutionary. Are you going to add me on it?"

"I'd rather eat my own poo. No offence."

Lila laughed, albeit with an 'eww' attached. It was only a matter of time before the groom, his mum or Lila's grandparents found us and split us up. I owed it to myself to get everything out of the system before that happened.

"Seeing you today is the best thing I've ever done," I said.

"Why?"

"Because I've never followed anything I care about through to its natural conclusion. I walk away, I get fired. I walked away from you."

"Without a proper goodbye, I might add."

"I thought I was being cool. Cool... What an idiot! Back then I thought *Hollyoaks* was cool!"

"Next time, fight for it. I've had to. And I've never been happier."

Lila and I shared a smile. If only there wasn't so much feeling and history there, we could have been great friends. But I had the feeling that this – in the words of our late, great mutual friend Jeffrey Scott Buckley – was our last goodbye.

Just to make sure the comfortable silence was broken into a million pieces, a Paris Hilton lookalike wearing huge sunglasses stumbled her way up to our table and practically threw herself onto Lila's lap, almost taking the table out as she threw her legs around to prevent herself from falling over.

"Wah! Bride of Chucky! Where the fuck have you been?" she said.

"Not only do sunglasses look really cool indoors, but they help you see better too," I said, attempting to prevent the table from collapsing under her weight.

"Get over it!" she said.

Good point, I thought. I didn't work here anymore. You can go through the fucking table for all I care. I stood up and decided that now was a good time to leave and rejoin my friends, who by now would be drunk and facing at least one sexual harassment charge.

Lila grabbed my hand with the only one she had free. Everything else was under the girl slumped across her.

"Please don't go. You haven't danced with me yet."

I paused, expecting there to be a punchline following that line.

"Are you forgetting the college socials? I never danced," I said.

"You danced with me," she said. "Right before you wandered into the toilets and declared your love for me."

"Weirdo!" The muffled voice of the girl called out from almost under the table.

"What a romantic bastard," I said.

"It was romantic. Now come and dance with me, or I'll never tell you what really happened with Steph."

My faced drained of all colour and a rush of panic shot up my spine.

"Just codding ya…" Lila said, in a shit Irish accent.

"Wedding or no wedding, I'm going to murder you for that!"

"Dance first. Murder later."

"Deal!" the drunk girl cried out again.

I leaned over the table and helped Lila put her drunk friend into an upright position. She wiped herself down and cuddled into Lila, who laughed and turned to me.

"Anyone would think that this day was for me," she said.

The girl muttered something incoherent. I chortled, which she didn't take kindly to.

"Don't take the piss out of me, you loser," she said, her eyes closed and her hair covering those awful sunglasses.

"No worries, Essex Hilton. Let's dance."

Lila and I walked back to the main area, accompanied by the walking advertisement for anti-binge drinking.

"Ready to show me those silky skills?" Lila asked.

"I have no skills. You know that. Which is why this is really mean."

"Maybe this is revenge for your first attempt at goodbye?"

"Ouch, you really know how to bear a grudge."

"You're goddamn right."

The girl finally broke away from Lila and faced us both. She looked more than a little confused, and after composing herself and belching, pointed at us both accusingly.

"You two have fucked each other, haven't you?"

Lila and I looked at each other, then back at the girl. I opened my mouth to say something stupid, but Lila beat me to it.

"Just now, actually, while you were attached to my leg."

"I'm very limber," I deadpanned.

The girl removed her sunglasses and looked at us closely.

"You two are weird," she said.

Bored with us, the girl wandered off towards the wedding bar area, and past Craig, who was keeping an eye on things and screwing over as many credit cards as possible, no doubt.

"What are you looking at?" The drunk girl said to him as she passed him.

Craig smiled at her, then looked over to me and nodded. I got the feeling that Conference Room Five was finally going to get christened tonight.

Lila laughed as she watched her drunk friend wander off.

"You do know that she's probably going to tell Mark about this?" I said.

"I don't care," she said. "He knows everything about me. Who I've slept with, who I've loved."

"Who have you loved?"

I couldn't help myself.

"Mark," she said, and purposely waited for a lifetime to say any more names just to torture me for being a nosey bastard.

"Tyler."

Tyler.

Wanker.

He was a guy who turned up in the second year of college. Everybody fancied him. He first came to college a metal fan, but within two minutes of realising that the girls were more into dance music, he switched to David Beckham highlights and yellow Pacha T-shirts. He was the first guy I ever felt jealous of around Lila, and as soon as we finished, he swept in.

"I can't believe you went out with Tyler. He was such a cock."

"Don't say that. Come and talk to him, he's much nicer these days."

Lila pulled me forward, and I froze.

"Oh Christ, he's here?"

"Nope," Lila said, trying to contain her wicked laughter with her hand.

"Absolute cow bag," I said.

"Oh, and Jason Chapman."

"It feels so good to hear you say that," I said.

Lila dragged me onto the dancefloor on our return, just as 'Don't Stop 'Til You Get Enough' was coming to an end. I managed to keep my Michael Jackson moves inside and opted for the bounce-on-the-spot-and-hope-that-the-song-ends-soon approach, which is a popular dance move amongst twenty-something white men with no rhythm.

The song changed to Duran Duran's 'Ordinary World', and I turned to walk away and leave Lila to her guests, but she grabbed my hand and pulled me towards her.

"My husband is at the bar, and I want to dance. So let's dance," she said.

I smiled and got into my best waltz position, which consisted of the exact same bounce on the spot moves, but holding a girl by the hand and the waist at the same time. I should have patented it really, I could've retired years ago.

Lila and I danced to the song in its entirety, and as clichéd as it sounds, it felt like it was our first dance. It wasn't until the song ended and Mark walked over and kissed his wife in front of me that I remembered that our time had passed, and this was just a sweet moment between two old friends.

15. Coming to Terms

The dancefloor was not the place for me, especially now that Lila and Mark were enjoying a dance together and almost everyone else was under 10 or over 50. I decided to quit while I was behind and find Sean and Jim instead.

I found them sitting in the far corner of the bar, accompanied by Amy and Dave. They cheered when I approached, and I spotted that Sean and Jim's eyes were closed from their alcohol intake.

"Hey buddy, how did the reunion go?" asked Sean.

"Better than I had any right to believe it would," I said.

Amy put a supportive hand on my back.

"I'm glad you got the chance to say your piece," she said.

"Me too," I said.

Jim sat upright in his chair, preventing himself from falling asleep and being kicked out by Craig or the night porters.

"Remember that guy she went out with after you? Tyler wasn't it? I loved that guy. Always had amazing hair."

Everybody nodded or grunted in agreement.

"Remember Lila's eighteenth birthday party at that pub in the middle of nowhere?" Sean asked.

"Oh my god, that was an amazing party!" said Amy. "You turned up and proclaimed your undying love for her. It was so romantic," she continued. "She told you that it wasn't the right time. You guys had no luck."

"I don't think luck had anything to do with it. I think that Lila was just meant to be with Mark. And if that's the case, then maybe there's somebody out there for me."

"Hear, hear," Dave agreed.

"What happened with that Helen girl you went on a date with?" Sean asked.

"Same situation," I said. "It just isn't the right time. I think Australia is the place for me. I've got some growing up to do."

"I think that's a sound way of looking at things, Jay," said Amy.

Jim stood up and necked a shot. He could barely stand.

"You're talking bullshit!"

But he could still swear.

Everybody was taken aback by Jim's sudden outburst, and he continued.

"I saw the way you were after you came back from that date with her. I've never seen you that happy before. If this girl is going to make you happy, fuck off the kangaroos and koalas and go and be happy. You bellend."

If Jim had stopped short of 'you bellend', I might have welled up. But this was Jim.

"He's right," said Sean, his eyes barely open. "My granddad always used to say, "If you love someone, set them free"."

"Your granddad never said that."

"No. No, he didn't. But it's true."

"Thanks, man."

Jim walked over to me, put his arm around me and ushered me to one side so that we could talk alone. Amy and Dave smiled and shook their heads as we stumbled off for a chat, and Sean started to fall asleep in his chair.

"Look man, if this girl means something to you, I want you to go for it. No regrets. I love you too much to see you miserable, and no matter how many Roo burgers you eat and how many INXS albums you listen to, you're still going to come back here. What happens if you miss the boat and this girl moves on? Because she will."

I let Jim's kind and thoughtful words sink in for a moment.

"I'll think about it. Let's just enjoy the rest of Lila's wedding first. OK?"

"Cool. Are you OK?"

"I'm fine. I feel really good actually."

"That's good news. I love you, man."

"I love you, too."

"You'd better, because I'm going to be building up expectations for you when I'm in Iraq, and if you disappoint me, I'll use your balls as a speed bag."

"Awesome."

"I'm glad we have an understanding."

Jim kissed me on the head, before swinging me back around so we could return to the table, where Sean was now asleep.

"Amy, pass me your lipstick. I'm going to have some fun," said Jim.

A reluctant Amy reached for her handbag, but sadly for Jim, Sean stirred.

"I'm awake. Just resting my eyes."

"Bastard," said Jim, his night ruined.

Amy turned and watched Lila and Mark dancing away. The dancefloor was almost empty.

"I feel like we need to give Lila some support," she said.

"Let's do it," Jim said.

We made our way to dancefloor, with Jim pulling a reluctant Sean to his feet. As we entered the main room, Lila and Mark came running towards us to drag us further into the dad dancing domain.

Sean grabbed Lila and started to dance with her, with Jim slapping Sean's behind as they danced. We all stood there laughing, and the DJ switched from Ultra Nate's 'Free' to 'The Love Shack' by The B-52s. There aren't many people in the world under the age of 90 who can resist the power of 'The Love Shack'. The song was practically invented for drunk people at parties to put aside their lack of natural rhythm and just say 'Fuck it, let's dance'. Everybody's moving and everybody's grooving, baby. Wise words.

The old college crew made the most of an almost empty dancefloor for three or four classic disco tracks, and as we boogied away, I considered what Jim had said about Helen. She had definitely made me happy, but with Molly, and then the wedding, I hadn't had the time to sit and think about her. Now I was thinking of nothing *but* Helen.

Helen was beautiful, intelligent, ambitious and kind, but I was only a couple of those things, and that could only create more trouble. What if we didn't work out? What if Molly grew attached to me and Helen ended up staying with me just to make her happy?

I made my decision, I was going to Australia, and I'd take my chances that Helen would still be single in a year's time. If only all of life's big decisions could be made whilst dancing to 'Crazy' by Gnarls Barkley.

I danced over to Jim and shouted in his ear.

"I love you, but I'm going to Australia."

Jim shook his head and continued dancing. I mimed 'I'm sorry' to him and he gave me his disappointed look.

Lila and Mark had started to slow down, and were doing that kissing and looking into each other's eyes thing that people in love do. They moved to the edge of the dancefloor and made their way towards the exit. I wasn't sure if they were coming back, but my heart seemed to think they weren't, which explained why it felt like someone had tied a ship's anchor to it.

I watched as they left, and as the song came to an end, a sobering and sympathetic Sean appeared at my side and put his hand on my shoulder.

"She's happy. Now it's your turn," he said.

I smiled, albeit with a heavy heart. Amy walked over to me and gave me a hug. It was clear that Lila wasn't coming back, and for the second time in five years, I'd missed out on a proper goodbye. I was just going to have to learn to move on without it.

The dancefloor started to fill up with the younger guests, and as Sean, Jim, Amy and Dave carried on dancing, I snuck out of the room and made my way through the hotel lobby. As I approached the main doors, I turned to see Craig and the drunk girl from earlier walking out of the lift. Craig smiled and held up five fingers. At least he could die happy now, I thought.

Before I could get off the hotel grounds, I heard the sound of bare feet slapping on the pavement behind me. I turned to see who the tiny steps belonged to.

Lila was standing there, holding her wedding dress up so that she could run and catch up to me.

"What the fuck?" I asked.

"Take me with you," she said, with a panic-stricken expression.

Before I could say a word, Lila broke into a huge smile, and the song I wrote for her all those years ago came flooding back, "I Love You (Almost as Much as I Want to Kill You)."

"You're evil," I said, my heart rate returning to normal.

Lila was grinning, and in that moment, I realised why we never worked all of those years ago, and why we could never be friends. She had left her new husband to come and mess with me one last time. Who does that? Maybe it wasn't just me who was emotionally immature. I thought back to the college years, and all the times that Lila made me angry, upset, jealous and filled with self-doubt. She hadn't changed a bit, and I was finally free.

"I thought that it would be a bit hypocritical of me if I left without saying goodbye."

"And without giving me heart failure?" I asked.

"I couldn't help myself. It seemed a little grandiose otherwise. Anyway, we owe each other this."

Lila stepped forward and kissed me gently on the forehead, both cheeks and then on the lips. I closed my eyes and felt my entire body release all of the anguish, regret and self-pity all at once. I pulled Lila close to me and held her tightly, and she whispered into my ear.

"Don't forget me. But don't let me hinder you."

Lila broke away from my embrace and smiled at me as she walked backwards to the hotel. We didn't take our eyes off each other until she turned to go back inside. I couldn't believe that she managed to walk back without tripping over her dress, but I was glad she made it, because it was a perfect moment.

I stood and stared into the lights of the hotel. A line of taxis appeared at the front entrance, and a light bulb turned on inside my head.

It was five minutes shy of midnight, but I was certain that Helen would still be up. I tried to call her as I approached one of the taxis, but her phone was switched off. I had no idea how I was going to get her attention without waking Molly up, but you don't think logically when you've got things on your mind and the urgency to get them out trumps your rational thought.

I opened the taxi door and asked if they were booked up. Fortunately for me, these taxi drivers were opportunists who figured that there would be drunk idiots needing a lift home or to their potential new girlfriends house. I hopped in the back and gave him the directions to Helen's house, sat back in the uncomfortable black leather seat and tried to get my blood pressure to a reasonable level.

In the movies, Hugh Grant – playing me in a career-best performance – would turn up at the door and sweep the girl off her feet, and any thoughts of Australia would become a distant memory. Sadly, the movie of my life was being directed by Ken Loach, which explained why I had no money, little hope and my pet bird was in the dustbin with a broken neck.

The taxi rocked up outside Helen's house, and I threw a £10 note at the driver. I must have been lost in love, because I'd never tipped a taxi driver in my life, even if it was only 75p. I tried calling Helen's phone again, but it was still turned off.

As I approached the front door, I noticed all the lights in the house were off. I knew there was a chance that I would wake Molly up, but I knocked on the door anyway. I stood back from the door so that I could see if any lights came on.

Nope.

Three more knocks, a little harder this time.

Nope.

Five knocks.

Success.

A light at the front of the house came on, which I assumed – and hoped – was Helen's bedroom, somewhere I was planning on spending a lot of time in the coming weeks, months and years.

My heart was thudding like tribal drums as the hallway light came on, and I could make out the silhouette of Helen coming towards the door. I stepped back, took a deep breath, and prepared for the grand romantic gesture.

The silhouette was not Helen. It was a man, and he was wearing a dressing gown. He looked pissed off, and big enough to kick my face in.

"Can I help you?"

"Who the fuck are you?" I asked, with all the machismo I could muster.

"It should be me asking you that, buddy. This is my house," he replied.

"You're Harry? Helen's ex-husband?" I asked, and I felt my stomach rise to my throat.

I was afraid to say anything else, in fear that my voice would break in front of the man who had clearly just come from Helen's bed. I backed away from the house, raising my hands in a 'please don't kill me' gesture. I might as well have just lied on the floor in front of him and started crying.

Helen walked down the stairs, also in her dressing gown, and called out to me.

"Jason, what are you doing here?"

Fuck you, Ken Loach, that's the second happy couple you've made me watch get together tonight.

"I don't know… I thought I knew," I said.

The road was looking really enticing right now.

Looking more than a little confused, Harry turned to Helen and pointed at me.

"You know this guy?"

"Can you give us a minute?" Helen said.

Harry went back inside the house, shaking his head in bemusement. I started to well up as Helen walked out of the house and approached me.

"I can't fucking believe it," I said, trying so hard not to scream the house down, and opting for an angry whisper instead.

"You can't believe what? That my ex-husband would sleep in the spare room occasionally to make the transition easier for Molly?"

The guilt and embarrassment hit me like a Ricky Hatton hook to the liver. I wanted to die.

"You're not…?"

"No. Go home."

All mums are armed with the 'I'm not angry, I'm disappointed' look, and it's a killer for anyone, especially hopeless romantics with no luck and who would now be stranded, not exactly sober, in an unfamiliar part of Leicester.

It was the second missed opportunity I'd watched walk away from me in the last thirty minutes. I wanted to stop her and tell her about Australia, and the fact that I chose her over the opportunity to travel, but the moment had passed. She entered the house and closed the door behind her.

I turned and left the driveway, making my way through a leafy area of Leicester that I'd visited only a handful of times. The streets looked like the maze in *The Shining*, but maniacal Jack Nicholson was replaced by my own feelings of being a dull boy, who deserved to be chopped to bits with an axe for being a moron.

It took me fifteen minutes to find London Road, which was nicely lit and led down to the train station, where I would be able to get a taxi back to my old house. I had to hope that Sean and Jim had opted to go straight home instead of venturing out to a nightclub.

I reached the taxi area at the train station and jumped into a black cab. It took all of my energy not to fall asleep in the back as we drove up to the house. I needed a break now. I needed the guys to be home.

They weren't.

The bastards.

The taxi prepared to leave, and I made the split-second decision to go to my parents'. I got back in and negotiated a £35 journey home. Who cares about money when you need a warm bed to sob yourself to sleep in?

I spent half of the taxi ride with my head in my hands, regretting the decision to turn up at Helen's house and getting the wrong end of the stick with her and the ex. There was no way that Helen was going to let me back in now, I had fucked it up. If I couldn't deal with the ex being in her life – even if it had been an honest mistake – then I had proven that Helen's fears were real: I wasn't emotionally mature enough to start a relationship with. I wrote and then deleted an apology text about five hundred times, before giving up and playing 'Snake II' instead.

I was barely awake when the taxi finally arrived at my folks' house, and as I handed over the last few notes I had in my wallet, all I could think about was crawling into bed and sleeping for a few weeks.

The taxi pulled away, and as I approached the house, a text message came through from Helen. I chose not to open it until I had the safety of my bed and a pillow to cry into like a big baby.

I crept through the house, which was pitch black, without any issues. Buckley – AKA 'the worst guard dog in the world' – was asleep in his basket and snoring like a drunk Brian Blessed, so I crept past him and up to my bedroom as quietly as possible.

I passed my parents' bedroom, and just before I entered my own, something drew me back to it. I noticed that the door was ajar, and I popped my head around the corner. Mum and dad were sound asleep, and they were spooning each other. I couldn't believe that dad had actually listened to me, but more than that, I was glad that an evening that had seen more ups and downs than a 70s porn shoot had come to a satisfying end, albeit not in the way that I had hoped for.

I stripped off and jumped into my bed. No matter how old you get, there is no better feeling than getting into a cold bed and excitedly wrapping yourself up in the quilt. It was awesome as a kid, and it would still be awesome in fifty years. I rolled onto my back and read the text message from Helen.

"ARE YOU OK?"

"EMBARRASSED. TIRED. STUPID. HAVE I MISSED ANYTHING OUT?" I replied.

I waited for a few moments, but fully expected Helen to be asleep by now.

"NO. I THINK YOU'VE COVERED IT."

Fuck.

I put my phone down next to me, but before I could doze off, it vibrated again.

"WHY DID YOU COME TO THE HOUSE?"

I wrote about forty replies – ranging from the truth to 'I dunno' – but in the end, I opted for a simple, "I MISSED YOU."

As soon as I hit the send button, I pictured Helen in bed, shaking her head at how stupid, immature and irresponsible I was.

I followed my text with another one, simply saying, "I HOPE I DIDN'T WAKE MOLLY UP. SORRY FOR BEING SUCH A MUPPET."

Helen didn't reply, and I took that as a sign that we were done.

Australia, here I come.

16. One Door Closes...

Waking up face-to-face with Buckley, who was watching me sleep like a psycho girlfriend, was a deserved punishment for being an impulsive moron, even though I had been berating myself for being the opposite for the past half a decade.

I checked my phone and saw that Helen hadn't been in touch in the six hours I had snoozed. I sighed, threw on a T-shirt and a pair of shorts, and headed downstairs to see the folks. Dad was outside in the garden, taking hours to mow a lawn that would take twenty minutes if he didn't stop every man and his dog who walked past the house for a chin wag.

Mum was reading the newspaper at the table, and I sat down and joined her. She was more than a little surprised to see me.

"Hello, stranger. What time did you get here last night?"

"About 2am, I think."

"Why didn't you stay at your old place?"

"It's a long story."

"OK. How did the wedding go?"

"Great. I ticked the boxes: saw the bride, talked to the bride, danced with the bride. And I didn't proclaim my undying love for her this time."

"Oh, that's good then."

Mum went back to her newspaper.

I hadn't eaten for ages, and having missed the evening buffet due to my binge drinking and soul-searching/vomiting session in the men's toilet, grabbed some Shreddies. Mum had purchased a coffee machine after watching dozens of American TV shows and movies where there is always coffee available. This was good news for me, as I would drink my bodyweight in the black stuff. I poured about three pints of coffee into Dad's huge fiftieth birthday mug, and rejoined mum at the table.

There was nothing mum hated more than lip-smacking. Dad would give entire lectures whilst eating, and it drove her crazy. I figured that I would get revenge on mum for not quizzing me more about my night by eating as loudly as I could whilst she tried to read the news.

It didn't take long for her to look up at me like Alex at the start of *A Clockwork Orange*.

"What?" I said, grinning in triumph.

"Did we not give you enough attention as a child?" she asked.

"Nope."

"That's a lie."

"I wanted to talk to you about my night."

"I thought you said it ticked all the boxes?"

"Yeah, but you were supposed to be intrigued. But instead you're reading an article about Paul McCartney turning 64."

"Newspaper editors have waited for over 40 years to write that headline. You can wait for my attention a little longer."

Mum was teaching me a well-deserved lesson, and I went back to my coffee and Shreddies. The post came through the front door, and I managed to hop from my seat and get to it before Buckley. I looked down at the sad mutt and shook my head.

"You're not too much use to me alive, are you?"

Buckley curled up in his basket and gave me a look that was half sadness and half choke-on-your-fucking-cereals.

I flicked through the post. One of the letters was addressed to me. The rest was junk, and I threw them onto Mum's newspaper just to be a brat, which raised a 'tut' out of her as she swept it aside.

I ripped open the envelope and scanned the letter. It was confirmation of my Australian working holiday visa.

Approved.

Get in.

Oh crap.

Now it was real.

"Fuck me," I said.

"Language."

"Sorry, Mum."

"What is it?"

"Acceptance of my application for a working holiday visa."

"You're definitely going then?"

Mum's response threw me off for a moment.

"Eh? Why wouldn't I?"

"Jim said that you'd met a nice girl, and that you'd had a good time together. He thought that you might stay and see where that went."

"Nah. That ship has sailed."

"Oh."

Mum went back to her newspaper, but I sensed that she wasn't too thrilled about the visa news. I put my hands on hers and she looked up at me.

"If you don't want me to go, I won't go. But aside from being here for you, I have nothing to keep me here."

Mum smiled at me.

"I would never want you to stay for me. I just want you to go for the right reasons. I don't want you to get out there, it not work out and you to come back a few weeks later because you hadn't thought it through."

Mum had a point, but I needed to get away. Lila's invitation was the shock that I needed to shake myself out of apathy, and everything that had happened since had taught me that I wasn't ready for a meaningful relationship and I needed to grow up.

"I know," I said. "But I need to get away for a while and figure out who I am and where I'm going in life. I can't do that here, and I can't do it living with Sean and Jim. I need to get out there and experience something different, and if it fails, it fails. But at least I'd have given it a shot. I've spent too long over the past few years thinking about stuff. Time to do some stuff."

Mum smiled again and squeezed my hands tightly.

"I am officially excited for you then," she said.

"Cheers, Momma," I said, and launched across the table to plant a kiss on her cheek.

"What's the next step?" She said.

"I guess I'll buy a lot of shorts and bright coloured T-shirts. Then I'll book my flights."

Taking a break from his strenuous lawn mowing activities, Dad entered the room and pointed to his birthday mug.

"Grab me one of those, chap," he said.

Mum and I shared a laugh at dad's expense.

"What are you two laughing at?"

"The fact that you're panting despite the fact that you've mowed the lawn for all of about eight minutes. I guess talking to the neighbours takes it out of you."

I went to the kitchen to get the old man a coffee, and had to duck dad's attempt to grab me by the scruff of the neck as I passed. I gave him his coffee and he raised a fist at me, which made me laugh.

"If you threw a punch at me, I could make dinner, wash up and then put you to sleep before it even landed. You're past your prime, old man."

"At least I had a prime, knobhead."

If some people overheard some of the conversations that took place between dad and I, or read a transcript, the police would be called immediately. But it was always in good spirits, and I was leaving those two in a far better place than they were before. I had spotted a few of mum's notebooks and business forms on dad's desk, which was a sign that they were going to work together this time. That bode well for my conscience while on the other side of the world.

"What have you got planned today?" Dad asked.

"I'm going to book my flight."

"Already? Wow, you're keen."

"May as well get it booked."

"You go for it, son. We're happy for you."

It was nice to hear him say that, and Mum looked up from her newspaper to give me a supportive wink and a smile. Everything was looking good.

I booked my flight from Heathrow to Brisbane via Singapore for Wednesday July 19, and the travel agent booked my first three nights in a hostel for me. I figured that if I was going to go backpacking, I should go the whole hog, and booked a hostel above a pub that stayed open until 4am, in a mixed dorm with 12 beds. The idea was to party through the jetlag, and destroy anything closely resembling the comfort zone on day one.

I went to Blacks and bought a £90 backpack, which was more than I'd spent on my suit, and then kitted myself out with some new trainers, T-shirts and shorts. It hadn't crossed my mind yet that it was 12 degrees and pissing it down in Brisbane. I was too caught up in the spirit of travelling to type "Brisbane weather" into Google.

Jim was flying out to Iraq a few days before I was due to leave for Brisbane, and we spoke on the phone the night before he left. Jim joked that he'd swapped our passport photos and plane tickets, and we were going to find ourselves in a *Trading Places* situation, but with more tanks and less comedy – although watching me fighting insurgents would probably be hilarious for some people.

"Are you scared? I'd have filled my pants by now," I asked.

"Nah, mate. I'm fine. I'm ready. I'm excited now."

"I will never understand how you do it. But I'm immensely proud of you, buddy. I'm proud to call you my friend."

"Thanks, buddy. That means a lot."

The sound of a toilet flushing interrupted my phone signal.

"Are you having a shit whilst having an emotional farewell?"

"I love you too, man."

The day before my flight, Sean and I met up for a coffee, and we were free to order the campest drinks on the menu now that Jim was fighting a war overseas instead of hanging out with his two idiot friends. We sat downstairs with the struggling novelists and chatted about Lila, the wedding and the future.

"Australia, man. You lucky bastard."

"I can't wait. It's going to be amazing."

"How do you feel about the whole Lila thing?" Sean asked.

"Who?"

Sean laughed and gave me the thumbs up.

"I feel good. Like you said, she's happy, now it's my turn."

"Exactly."

"Did Jim tell you what happened the day before he left to join his regiment?"

"Go on..."

Sean shook his head in disbelief before telling the story.

"He went back home to his folks house for a while, and being Jim, he couldn't just spend time with his family before going to fight a war. He had to go out, get pissed and get laid. He came home at night with some girl and then sent his five-year-old sister into the room the next morning to find out what her name was. The little sweetheart walked into the living room giggling, wearing a gimp mask she'd found. Jim's parents were fucking mortified."

"As am I... What did Jim do?" I asked.

"He took a picture of his sister wearing the mask and giving the thumbs up. It's now his MySpace profile picture."

"That's our war hero," I said.

"He's a walking advertisement for birth control."

We finished our coffees, headed upstairs and out into the street. The awkwardness started to set in as we realised this would be the last time we'd see each other for at least a year.

"I'm going to miss you, man. You've always been the voice of reason," I said.

"Don't go soppy on me now."

"I mean it. Thank you for everything."

"I didn't do anything. If anything, you should be thanking Lila. If she hadn't invited you to the wedding, we'd be sitting at home playing Fight Night and ordering pizza."

"And I'd be employed."

"Exactly. Thank fuck for Lila Holmes."

"Lila *Shattersby*," I said.

Awkward silence.

We shuffled on the spot for a moment, like two kids meeting behind the Humanities block for our first kiss, before I took the initiative and gave Sean the squeeze of all squeezes. He patted me so hard on the back that I could taste my vanilla latte all over again.

"Stay in touch," he said.

"I will."

"When you get back, we'll have the piss-up to end all piss-ups."

"Of course."

We went our separate ways, me to get the train home in preparation for the big departure, and Sean to start searching for a new place to rent, as a three-bedroomed house with no good furniture but too many memories was no longer ideal for him. We kept turning back and waving to each other every few moments until we turned a corner.

A few months ago, if anybody had seen me come home from work, pick up an Xbox controller and share a beer with my two friends, they would never have predicted we'd be in the positions we were in now.

Lila's invitation had done much more than send me on a path to acceptance via a downward spiral. It had been the wakeup call for all three of us, and it would ultimately save our friendship.

We were no longer relying on each other and living out of each other's pockets.

It would take some getting used to, but at least Sean's socks would be lighter.

Dad offered to drive me to the airport, and it made sense to say yes. As much as I love public transport, I didn't fancy lugging a backpack around on a three hour train journey where I'd be lucky to get a seat, not to mention the London underground and everything else I would need to get to Heathrow. Basically, I'm a lazy bastard.

Mum decided not to come with us. She told me that she couldn't stand sitting in a car with me for all that time, knowing that I'd be leaving her for a year. She slipped an envelope filled with Australian dollars into my backpack and gave me a hug at the door. I looked back at her as she stood in the door waving, and as worried as I was about her, I felt like she would be OK now that dad was tuned in to what was going on with her.

"She's going to miss you, you know," Dad said, loading my backpack into the boot. "We didn't see much of you before, but we knew you were only 45 minutes away if you needed us. I think it's going to hit her hard when she realises she won't have that luxury for a year."

"She'll be fine. She's got you to look after her."

"Oh I'm sure that's a huge comfort to her!" Dad laughed.

"You'd be surprised."

We pulled out of the driveway and made our way to the main road. I kept waving to mum until the house was out of sight, and then turned my attention to dad's CD collection. He had solid taste in music and films, and we opted for *Chutes Too Narrow* by The Shins.

"Did you get an iPod for all your music? You're going to need it. Every time we went to the beach as a kid you got restless after five minutes," said Dad.

"I'll be fine, Dad."

"Just saying."

The car journey breezed by as Dad and I indulged in some great music and chatted about old times. My paranoia had started to set in, and I kept checking my pockets to see if my wallet, passport and ticket were still there, as if some gremlin could have found its way into the car and stolen them. I muttered "Wallet, passport, ticket" to myself as I checked my pockets, like a mental patient creating their own version of 'Head, shoulders, knees and toes'.

They were still there.

Every time.

We pulled into a space at the drop-off section of the airport.

"Well, here we are," Dad said. "I don't need to ask if you've got everything, do I? I'll be saying 'Wallet, passport, ticket' to myself all the way home. Thanks for that."

"You're welcome," I laughed.

"Give your old man a hug then," he said.

Cars were not designed for awkward man hugs, but we just about managed it, even if the gear stick managed to embed itself between my ribs as I leant across.

"Love you, mate. Have a great time. Ring me when you need picking up… and other times throughout the year, obviously."

"Cheers, Dad."

"Now get out of my car so I can put Dire Straits on."

We shared a laugh, and I jumped out of the car and grabbed my backpack from the boot. I slammed the boot down and made my way to the airport doors, taking my phone out of my pocket and turning it on.

I turned back at the doors and waved dad off. I could hear that Dire Straits was now on the stereo, and twice as loud as before. When I was little, Dad had a banged out old Fiesta, a radio that couldn't pick up a signal, and one tape: Dire Straits. He played that thing to death, and almost drove mum and me to insanity with it. How he could still listen to it without driving his car into a brick wall was a mystery to me.

I was about to enter the airport when the phone rang.

It was Helen.

Fuck.

Bad timing.

I let it ring out, knowing that I had deactivated the voicemail option ready for travelling overseas. Chances were that the phone would die at some point during the year as it was older than the pyramids. I had written down the numbers I wanted to keep so that I could get in touch with people on my return.

The phone rang again.

Against my better judgement, I answered.

I was met with the voice of an extremely cute eight-year-old girl.

"Hello. Jason? It's Molly."

I felt a mixture of emotions as that sweet voice came through my crappy device.

"Hi Molly, how are you?"

"Good. Mum talks about you a lot. I think she misses you," she said, with the blunt honesty only a kid can pull off.

"Really? That's nice."

I had no idea what to say. I'd never been set up by a child before.

"When are you coming over again? I'm on the Valley of Bowser now. Can't do the Ghost House."

I closed my eyes and smiled. Damn, this girl is adorable, I thought. There was nothing I wanted to do more than to go over to the house, complete that level and give the little monkey an explanation and a proper goodbye, even if she probably wouldn't understand.

"I don't know, Molly. I don't think…"

In the background, I could hear Helen telling Molly off for using her phone. Molly muttered something that I couldn't make out, and then the line went dead.

The phone rang again.

Helen.

I answered the phone, expecting it to be Molly asking me how to complete Bowser's Castle.

It was Helen this time.

"Hello?" I said.

"Hi, it's me. I wanted to apologise for Molly ringing you."

"That's fine," I said.

"Are you alright?" she asked.

"Never better."

"Where are you?"

"Home… I'm at home."

"What Molly said, about me missing you… She was telling the truth. I do miss you."

Kill me.

"Do you miss me?" she asked.

Shoot me in the face and bury me in the surrounding fields.

"Jason, do you miss me?" she asked again.

Fill a bathtub with hydrofluoric acid and fetch me my swimming trunks.

"Jason? Jason…? Are you there?"

Good question.

Am I here?

The airport was right in front of me.

I had a ticket. Paid in full.

I would be in the sky within three hours, on the other side of the world within 24.

I had spent 23 years running away from responsibility and relationships. Why stop now?

The automatic doors of the airport had opened and closed a thousand times in the time that I had been standing in front of them, but now they stayed open, as if they were somehow willing me to make my bid for freedom.

I looked down at my phone, which still had Helen's voice coming from it, and back up to those open airport doors that were calling my name.

Should I stay or should I go?

I took a deep breath, closed my eyes, and made my decision.

Acknowledgements

Special thanks to Sarah, Tim, Daniel, my folks and family, my friends, my imaginary friends, my therapist, my dealer, my masseuse, the DMU class of 2012 and all my tutors.

A huge thank you to Lex, Cate and Hope for their honest and often brutal editing.

To the people and establishment owners of Leicester and Rutland: Please don't sue me.

If you made it this far, cheers for reading.

Daley James Francis will return.

I've always wanted to write that.

Printed in Great Britain
by Amazon.co.uk, Ltd.,
Marston Gate.